Freeport Public Library
Freeport, Illinois

McGarr and the Legacy of a Woman Scorned

A VIKING NOVEL OF MYSTERY AND SUSPENSE

Also by Bartholomew Gill

McGarr and the P. M. of Belgrave Square
McGarr and the Sienese Conspiracy
McGarr on the Cliffs of Moher
McGarr at the Dublin Horse Show
McGarr and the Politician's Wife
McGarr and the Method of Descartes

McGarr and the Legacy of a Woman Scorned

Bartholomew Gill

VIKING

VIKING
Viking Penguin Inc., 40 West 23rd Street,
New York, New York 10010, U.S.A.
Penguin Books Ltd, Harmondsworth, Middlesex, England
Penguin Books Australia Ltd, Ringwood, Victoria, Australia
Penguin Books Canada Limited, 2801 John Street,
Markham, Ontario, Canada L3R 1B4
Penguin Books (N.Z.) Ltd, 182–190 Wairau Road,
Auckland 10, New Zealand

First published in 1986 by Viking Penguin Inc.
Published simultaneously in Canada

LIBRARY OF CONGRESS CATALOGING IN PUBLICATION DATA
Gill, Bartholomew, 1943–
McGarr and the legacy of a woman scorned.
I. Title.
PS3563.A296M26   1986   813'.54   85-40627
ISBN 0-670-80673-0

Printed in the United States of America by
The Book Press, Brattleboro, Vermont
Set in Caledonia

McGarr and the Legacy of a Woman Scorned

1

McGarr glanced up and tried to remember where he had seen the object clutched in the dead woman's hands.

Across the attic window at the top of the stairs, a cloud as dense as a splotch of black ink passed, and the pane rattled in its jamb. The house was damp, cold, and forbidding now at dusk. The cat that had been found sleeping near the corpse brushed against his leg.

McGarr looked down again. It was a bottle but not a bottle. The bottom had been cut off but precisely, using hot water and a string, and it was that open end which sounded some resonance in his memory. There was some use for the bottle that the long, thin fingers clasped, but he could not recollect what.

A fall? An accident?

McGarr studied the iron-gray waves flecked with silver, the deep blue eyes that had glassed over in death, the long, well-structured face and thin, aquiline nose. Having fallen cleanly down the steep flight of stairs, she had come to rest on her stomach and chest. Her neck was bent oddly to the side, so the chin was touching a shoulder. One foot still lay on the final stair.

Why cleanly, he thought? She could have tumbled first. There was a gash on her left forearm, a bruise on her left cheek, but she had broken her neck in the fall, he suspected, here at the bottom of the stairs. How old, he wondered? Late fifties, early sixties. She had been a well-built, fit-looking woman with lightly tanned skin and full lips pulled back slightly in an expression that reminded McGarr of the first movement of a smile.

She was wearing a pleated, flower-print dress made of some thin material, befitting the season, and McGarr wished his wife had accompanied him when the phone call had come through. They were on their summer holidays at his father-in-law's estate in nearby Kildare, and the dress that the victim was wearing looked costly, even chic. Then the sheen on her patent-leather sandals told him they were new. Had she dressed for somebody? Had she expected a caller?

As well, the entire "feel" of the place—from the flounced curtains to the doilies on every chair—was feminine, to say nothing of the two sisters of the victim and a niece, who had told him they'd be in the sitting room if he wanted them. And it disturbed him now that, in spite of the well-lit spaciousness of the large Edwardian house on a stormy, high summer evening, he found its atmosphere oppressive.

Glancing at Stack, the Gárda superintendent from Rosslare Harbor, McGarr eased the cat aside and climbed the Oriental runner toward the attic. There on this final reach of the three-story house, the rug looked almost new—just another thing in the house that had been costly in its time and had been . . . conserved, as in a kind of museum. There had been no muddy boots on that carpet, no children, no dogs. Nobody smoking a pipe or a cigar or even, he judged (albeit unfairly), a cigarette. What was it about the place that was bothering him so?

But at the top of the stairs, the frilled end of the rug was tented up, so that the heads of brass tacks, newly removed from the seal of varnished wood, gleamed even in the dim light from the attic. McGarr slipped a woven-leather brogue into the cup that it formed, and tried to lift up. Although held by only one tack on one end and two on the other, the rug trapped his foot until, stepping down on a stair, he tugged and an end popped free.

A short, well-built man with strong legs, McGarr wondered at the force necessary to have pried up—how many? He counted them—six tacks, though some may have been dislodged before she snagged her foot.

Clear bare bulbs, dim and coppery, had been arranged over banks of wooden boxes and trunks, three of which had recently been opened for the first time in years. McGarr played the beam of his penlight across the surface within and noted how, like snow in flurries, dust had fallen as the lids had been raised. Swirled patterns lay over the dull, yellowed satin of an old wedding dress, its lace crumbling. Below it, he could see most of a wedding portrait, the bride and groom.

It was the dead woman herself when young and haughtily fetching, he concluded, though she had been described to McGarr as *Miss* Walton by Stack, to whom she had been known as a spinster. "Fionnuala and Dan," the caption read, "6th June, 1947."

In the two other trunks were letters and photos and leather-bound notebooks, some with clasps and dates that looked like diaries. There was a family Bible with "Walton" in raised Gothic and leather letters across the bottom. Somebody had rummaged through them, looking for something. One was still open, and nearly all—McGarr could tell from the age marks on their covers—had been disturbed. He touched nothing.

Instead he reached for a Woodbine, the thin, cheap cigarettes which he had smoked since he had been a child. In the flicker of a match his face seemed long and even now with a suntan somewhat drawn. Just at his mid-century, McGarr was Chief Superintendent of the Murder Squad of the Gárda Síochána, the Irish police. Red hair fringed the sides of an otherwise bald head, and he turned eyes, which were the palest of gray, to the window.

It was a boxed, Edwardian window, large with multiple panes, that looked out on a well-tended front lawn. Beyond a hedge, a gravel drive dropped steeply through treeless pastureland toward the array of lights at Rosslare from which car ferries now connected Ireland to Fishguard in Wales and Le Havre on the Continent. Out on the long crescent of seawall that fronted Wexford Harbor, waves were crashing, sending up spumes of spray that seemed almost crystalline in the encroaching darkness.

To the southwest, nearly as far as the eye could see, lay a storm-tossed expanse of planted fields broken only by hedgerows and a windbreak of ancient chestnut trees that —he assumed—girded some farmhouse. On the periphery of the grove stood five metallic silos with the half dozen barns and as many outbuildings that serviced the spread nearby.

McGarr stepped yet closer to the window. He tugged on the Woodbine and listened to the wind keening through the slates. From there he could see across the gables to the northeast and the scrub of pitch, punctuated dimly by the light of Tuskar Rock, which was St. George's Channel. Somewhere not far from the house the Irish Sea was raging, each roller booming on the strand.

Turning back, McGarr paused to survey the contents of the room. What had he been seeing? Or not seeing?

Dust—what so totally covered the tops of unopened trunks seemed to be missing from the floor. He bent and wiped his palm across the rough, deal boards that were different from the tight-grained maple of the attic landing, the stairs, and the hall below.

"I noticed that as well, chief," said Stack. "Swept clean. Every place but here." With the barrel of a ballpoint pen, the slightly built, uniformed officer swung back the door, which was recessed. He looked down at the space made where it met the wall. Like a median, a single footprint divided the triangle of dust there.

"A woman's foot," he went on, "About size four."

Five, thought McGarr.

"The victim has nines," Stack went on, his scrubbed skin pulled so tight over his old face that he looked priestly and officious.

Sixes, thought McGarr. Stack must have opened the strap of the sandal with the barrel of the pen and read the number upside down.

"Round toe, that," he went on, checking off something in his notebook, obviously the information he had compiled before phoning Dublin Castle.

Square, McGarr amended silently. The print only appeared rounded because the woman who had stood there had placed her weight on the ball of her foot as she strained to reach up toward the implements on the wall. A small woman, five feet. Perhaps five feet two. Tops.

Then the tools on the wall seemed like antiques of sorts. Of the eleven items there, McGarr's admittedly urban eye could identify only a much-worn sickle, a farrier's hammer, and a cooper's brace.

But like the floor, the wall too had recently been dusted.

With wide, sweeping strokes, the area up to three or four inches above the hooks had been wiped clean. Then the cobwebs had been batted from the hooks, and every piece carefully rehung save the last device.

It looked to McGarr like a nail-puller or a small, foot-and-a-half long carpenter's wrecking bar, which had not been replaced with the same care as the other tools. It was a solid piece of forged steel, and heavy, from the look of it.

And what was he seeing? Careful of the footprint, McGarr stepped in toward the wall and raised his five-foot-eight-inch frame up on his toes. Removing a penlight from his jacket, he played the narrow beam over the stout claw of the tool.

On it was a smudge or a stain, and he was tempted to lift the object off the wall, the better to examine it under a light, but he forebore. Patience. Yes, he was on holiday and most assuredly the call from Dublin with the neutral, nasal, and mutedly nasty voice of a new Assistant Commissioner, wondering if McGarr couldn't just "pop down and look see," had come as something of an imposition, since Dunlavin in Kildare was at least fifty miles to the north.

At first he had thought the man—some politician's son with only a thin legal background in a discipline called Constitutional Law—had merely been trying to assert his authority, until he added, "Friends of mine in the area, and the less made of it the happier I'll be." The capability of providing for that man's happiness had not until that moment occurred to McGarr, and it rather piqued his interest that a possible murder could be considered a matter of friendship.

Then, two weeks of vacation had always been quite enough for McGarr, and after seventeen straight days at his father-in-law's horse farm he was more than simply restless. How so many grown and not unintelligent adults could converse so unremittingly about certainly handsome and useful but essentially dumb and unavailing beasts, like horses, had by day three become a subject of some speculation to McGarr.

Was there a life out of the saddle? Surely in the barn or the paddock and—because of the family's other interest, which was art—in the study, but the purview of that family, which in every other way McGarr held dear, was too narrow and specialized for his tastes. A Dubliner born and bred, he himself required multiplicity, diversity, and difference, and, to be honest, there was only so much fresh air and wholesome living that he could take at one go.

Glancing down at the cigarette, which was his first since he began the holiday and tasted perhaps better than any he had ever smoked, McGarr pointed to the misplaced tool in the top row of those that had been hung behind the attic door. "Ever see something like that before?" he asked Stack, the uniformed superintendent.

"Sorry to say I'm not from these parts myself. I mean, sorrh. I'm sorry here and now to say that I'm not—"

McGarr raised a hand to signal that he had understood. Stack's deep blue uniform was so neat and his face so clean and closely shaven that the unbroken bushy line of his eyebrows seemed absurd and theatrical. They were twitching. "At'lone," he said by way of explanation, meaning the Midlands city in County West Meath. The twitching ceased.

The Gárda was a national police force, and its officers were frequently transferred. In a country in which family and clan still mattered most, it made for a more evenhanded administration of the law, if at some cost.

Cupping the Woodbine in his left hand, McGarr moved

through the doorway but stopped at the rug at the top of the stairs. There he hunkered down and played the beam of the penlight over the surface of the varnished floor where the nails had pulled free.

There, as he had suspected, the slick surface had been scratched by some tool and even marred slightly where the fulcrum of the claw had swiveled slightly as force had been exerted to pry up the tacks. Brass, they would have left traces on the instrument, which in no way, however, accounted for the smudge—some liquid that had dried brown—that he had noticed on the head of whatever object it was which had been misplaced there behind the door.

Standing again, he glanced down the stairs at the victim and the gash on her left forearm. Had she raised it to fend off an attacker? Had he also struck her on the cheek? Why *he?* McGarr thought of the footprint in the dust, that of a woman smaller, at least in bone structure, than the victim.

Shifting his head slightly, he squinted through the encroaching darkness at the object clutched in her hands and suddenly remembered what it was or at least what he suspected it to be. A "blower," a device that he had heard —how many years ago, twenty or so?—had been used by people in the Wexford area to object to any marriage that the community deemed improper: to a Tinker or to somebody too old or deformed or too closely related or held in general disrepute. Marriages between persons of differing religions had also been "blown upon," he could remember having heard, and even those in which property was involved, when a new alliance might alter the expectations of a large or powerful family.

Then young men would gather at crossroads or near the homes of the intended and bleat and wail late into the night through the bottomless bottles, which in ancient times had been rams' horns. The sound was like none other, McGarr had been told, a shrill, grating complaint that made sleep impossible and continued night after night until the parties relented. Those who defied the judgment, which was not lightly disposed, were considered pariahs and treated as such. In a rural setting it was a curse that could make life impossible, and it gave McGarr pause to consider how both brutal and effective had been the enforcement of the informal, pre-British moral codes of the country.

"Anything missing?" McGarr asked Stack, as he stepped over the raised end of the rug and moved down the carpeted stairs.

"Nothing, sir, though the niece who found her claims no knowledge of the attic and them trunks. Locked, they were—the attic, the trunks—and the key kept by the victim and dispensed to nobody else.

"Miss Fionnuala Walton, she was," Stack went on, flipping a page in a worn vinyl notebook. "Mistress of Greenore House. Here. Age, sixty-two or thereabouts, according to her two sisters, Siobhan and Machala, who also live on the premises. Founder and proprietress of Greenore Eugenics, the horse breeders."

Even McGarr remembered the name in connection with several six-figure sales of thoroughbred foals to foreign parties—sheiks or oil magnates or the like. The papers had been full of it, the auction having been, as he remembered, in Dublin during the Horse Show some years ago. By comparison his wife's father's operation in Kildare was tiny.

"Owner?" he asked.

Stack's eyebrows bunched. "I'm afraid I wouldn't know that either, sir, though local gossip has it that she's got bags of money. Bags and bags," he averred.

"The farm buildings there to the west?" McGarr meant the complex that he had glimpsed out the attic window. They were standing over the victim again, looking down at her.

"I wouldn't say so, sir. I believe they're to the south between here and Churchtown." It was the small village between Greenore and Carnsore Points, and McGarr made note that he should consult the map that he had in his car. Wexford, which was known as the Sunny Southeast, had been for him, as for so many other Irish, a favorite holiday spot before he had met his wife, but he had not been back for nearly a decade. Even if Greenore Eugenics were a failing concern, ownership of any amount of land near the broad and often sandy beaches could be worth a sizable packet of money, here where the days were bright and the sun sometimes hot.

"Who had access to the house?"

Stack flipped a page. "Summers, like this, with all the holiday-makers about, they keep the doors locked. Place large as this and set off looks like a hotel or at least a guesthouse. There's signs down by the gate, which Miss Fionnuala was thinking of making electronic, though she was grousing over the expense. Says she to me—"

"Keys," McGarr interrupted. "Perhaps you'd best tell me about the keys and who had them. Front door and back." With half a county living in his ear, the rural policeman usually became an inveterate gossip. It was, McGarr supposed, an occupational affliction, though he knew men who possessed a priestly reticence in that regard.

The voices of several women and a man rose to them from somewhere on a lower floor of the large house. Sounds only, no words intelligible.

With the implied rebuke, Stack squared his narrow shoulders and pressed his chin close to his chest. "Apart from the victim's key, which can be seen among those there on her belt, I make it that only the two sisters have keys and the niece, Deirdre Walton, who's here for the summer and her impending marriage and"—he expelled some breath—"who knows how long.

"But I was told by the niece herself, now, that two others exist. One is held by Tom Daugherty, who's manager at Greenore Eugenics, the other by his brother Dan Junior, the"—there was another slight pause—"espoused.

"I found both doors, front and back, locked when I arrived. I had to knock . . . *bang* before I was let in. The grievin' and all, I suppose.

"Says the niece, she says, 'Certainly I didn't try to lock you out. The latch here, like you can see, is on.' Says I, 'How long was it, after you discovered the body, that you rang me up?' " Stack flipped a page. " 'Why—immeegitly, you fool, since she was still alive. I thought you might be able to supply some medical aid.' " Stack glanced up at McGarr and then down at the body. "Her pulse was flickering, I'd say, but"—he shook his head, as if to say that there could have been no help for the woman.

"I straightaway dropped everything and called hither and yon for the doctor, who I could find nowhere. I tried some others, but nothing, and I decided that with the new patrol car and all I could rush her to the hospital . . . but by then her soul had flown, so it had. God rest her soul.

"I was here maybe a quarter hour, when his nibs" — Stack motioned his head to the sound of the man's voice from below—"arrived and confirmed my opinion. It was then that he began whatever it is he's doing for the others. I myself climbed the stairs, and seeing what I did, I posted some boys on the doors, told them downstairs nobody was to leave the house, and I called Dublin. I only hope I did right."

McGarr reached out and touched his sleeve. "Did he move her?"

"The doctor?"

McGarr nodded.

"I don't believe so. It was his first concern—that none of us had. Neck broke, said so himself, and not a breath in her then. Nor a beat."

A door shuddered open on a floor below and crashed into its stop. An obviously distraught female voice inveighed, "I must be with her. Now and until. . . . You know how she hated to be alone. My one concern is that she—her spirits—have gone someplace where . . . there are no others."

"Please, Siobhan, you know she didn't believe in that bunk," said another woman's voice.

"And the police are still here." The third woman's voice was young and almost musical in quality. It was high in tone and light; it lilted.

"*Are* they still here?" Siobhan asked.

Said a man, obviously the doctor, "Yes, dear—they haven't finished their investigation."

"*Investigation?*" she cried. "What in the name of all that's holy could they possibly have to investigate? The poor woman. . . ." Her voice cracked, and she began to sob.

Said the calmer of the two older voices, "Deirdre— can't you go up to them? It might be important to know what *they* plan."

"Plan what?" the distraught one objected, her voice fading as she was being led away.

"With Fionnuala, of course, and you should get yourself

used to the idea. The police being here could mean almost anything." The other woman's sobbing diminished, as she was led into some other room. They heard a shuffle of feet and the closing of a door.

Suddenly a small young woman appeared at the top of the stairs. She was pretty, with dark black and wavy hair and an oval, tanned face that made more emphatic the appearance of her eyes. They were the very color of the sea water pooling over an ivory beach that McGarr had glimpsed while driving up the hill toward Greenore Point. He imagined that in shadow they were gray, in direct sunlight almost green.

They widened imperiously, as she surveyed Stack and McGarr, then looked down at the dead woman on the floor. She blinked and said, "We're wondering when you'll be through here. You can imagine that we're anxious to notify the funeral director in Wexford, and, as it's getting late—" She snapped up her wrist but did not glance at her watch. "Who is this man, Superintendent?"

She was wearing a plain black dress, belted at the waist. Her body, though diminutive, was angular, her legs shapely. On her small feet were flat, colorfully beaded shoes with square toes.

"I'm with the Gárda as well," said McGarr, stepping toward her before Stack could respond with McGarr's title. "Dublin. I was in the neighborhood, so to speak, and the Superintendent here asked me to stop by."

"And—?" Perhaps it also had something to do with her bearing, which was erect and even militant, but the way she tilted back her head and looked down her long, slightly beaked nose made McGarr feel smaller than she.

"A tragedy," he went on, turning awkwardly to the corpse. "A shame. D'y'know that eighty-foive parcent of accidents resulting in grave bodily injury or hospital care occur either in the home or within a ten-mile radius therefrom?" His eyes widened and they held her icy gaze until she finally blinked. "Which is small consolation for you, I know. I know. But—"

"When, pray, will you make an end? I hope you can understand it's all I want to know. I have my aunts—" She gracefully swung a hand toward the staircase, as though showing them out.

In caricature now, McGarr sighed. He shook his head and again considered the corpse. "Ah, well—now that the Gárda's here there're a few formalities which must be observed, I'm afraid. It was you who called us, if I'm not mistaken?"

"What formalities?"

McGarr scratched an eyebrow, knowing that his forehead would wrinkle high onto his bald head. He was in a partial stoop, and he noticed that her thighs, bound in the tight black dress, bore the hard muscles of a horsewoman. "We ourselves are off now, but the Technical Squad should be arriving directly."

"But—" Stack began to say, when McGarr's hand slipped around his bicep and grasped him with some force.

"The Technical Squad? What is *that?*"

Did McGarr see the condescension in her delightfully colored eyes crumble? He thought he did. And how old could she be, he wondered? Twenty . . . two at most. The tanned, olive tones of her skin still enjoyed the smooth, unwrinkled textures of a child, fuzzed lightly on the nape of her neck by fine blond hairs.

"And this is a *crime* scene," she said in a flat tone that communicated all the more her intended sarcasm. "Since when, you'll have the goodness to tell me, is it a crime to plummet headlong down a staircase and"—her eyes shied and then suddenly flooded with tears—"break one's neck?

Here my great-aunt lies. And from *there"*—in a fluid motion she turned and pointed to the top of the stairs— "she fell." A tear burst from her eyes and fell on the back of McGarr's right hand. The tendons in her neck were taut, her pulse there throbbing, and McGarr had not placed her accent. Like the other, older voice he had heard speaking in the hallway of a lower story, it was Irish but vaguely, as though she had taken elocution lessons or lived abroad for some time. "Do you need to know more than that?"

McGarr cocked his head. "Ah, but we do."

"When, in that case, can we get her off this blasted floor?"

McGarr asked himself what, apart from the shape of her shoes and her manner, which could easily be explained by a certain immaturity, made him think that her performance here was histrionic?

Surely she had cause to complain. He would not have allowed his own aunt to lie there at the pleasure of the police and for at least two hours more, if he now had his way.

Was it her readiness to confront them? Her attractiveness? Her accent? "Of course—then there's the pathologist," he said.

Stack's head moved to the side. He lowered the notebook and looked away.

McGarr again took his arm. "Well, we're off now. On holiday meself." He winked at the woman. "Like I said, the others 'll be by soon. I must advise you not to touch anything. It'd be better still if you joined your . . . is it, aunts?"

Her unusual eyes were still fiery.

"We'll see ourselves out," McGarr continued, leading

Stack toward the door. To him, he said, "Your men must be tired. Sure, the Squad will be here any moment now, and you can tell them all to go home."

"But isn't it a bit ex—"

McGarr silenced him, saying, "Wisht, now. We must not forget ourselves."

When the door to the entry was closed, he turned to Stack and said, "You've acquitted yourself well here, Superintendent, and there's a reason, you'll see, for what just went on in there. Now come closer while I tell you what I've got in mind, and I want you to follow my orders to the letter. First, I want you to get one of your men to drive my car away. You can leave it down by the gate.

"Then, is there some place close-by a person can put up for the night?"

Stack canted his head. "All of Wexford is booked up solid, this time of year, but there's the odd farmhouse accommodation. Sometimes Mna Daugherty takes in a guest or two."

"Related to this Tom and Dan Daugherty Junior?" McGarr asked.

"Their mother. It's the big farm across the road, about a mile distant."

"And they live there?"

"Tom does, sure. But not Dan Junior. Him and the mother don't get on at all, at all. Dan's got a room in the stables at the Eugenics where he works, I've heard. Groom."

"Where's that notebook of yours and your pen? There's a number in Kildare I want you to call, and I'll jot down what I want you to say . . ."

After he heard Stack and the others depart, McGarr waited several minutes, his ear nearly pressed to the door leading into the Edwardian structure. Panes of multicolored, leaded glass in floral and heraldic patterns enclosed the entry, and the pale glow to the west told him that the short, Irish summer night was nearly upon them.

Hearing nothing, he eased open the door and, feeling almost foolish, like a child playing a game, he stepped back into the house. Careful to tread only the wall side of each staircase, he climbed quickly and silently up past the dead woman and into the thin, amber light of the attic.

There in the shadow of a chimney, he batted the dust from an old storage box. He then sat, wishing he might smoke but knowing he could not. It would make that second cigarette taste all the better, he told himself. And then, he had brought along his flask.

2

Minutes went by—five, ten—
in which McGarr listened to the wind soughing through
the eaves. In gusts it rose to a moaning lament that was
lugubrious and elegiac and, he judged, appropriate to the
occasion. It complained to him of desolation and life loss
and the pointlessness of an individual human life, when
weighed against a universe that could give rise to such a
sound. When the lament died he believed he could hear
the dust sifting through the shaft of pale light a foot in
front of him.

Glancing up at its solid oak timbers, McGarr reflected
on the ambience of the house itself that was better suited
to, say, a residential neighborhood in Dublin or London
than the nearly treeless, windswept hills beyond the tiny,
cobwebbed window near his shoulder. It was one of those
places that, set off on its own and seen from afar, made a
person wonder who lived there and what life from that
prospect could be like. Spectacular, as now in summer, it
was for much of the year—McGarr did not doubt—a bar-
ren and forbidding place, especially for three childless
spinsters, should Stack's allusion be correct. Then, of
course, there was the niece.

Turning his head to the open trunks, he caught sight of the lacy fringe of the wedding gown and the ruffled brim of a flounced hat. He raised his eyes to the object, which he now remembered the name of, that had been hung carelessly behind the door, then to the whorls high on the wall where the dust had been removed. There was, of course, the footprint below and the trunk with all the diaries and journals that had been disturbed for the first time in years.

It was a farrier's claw, an antique tool.

It made him think of the blower, which was still clutched in the victim's lifeless hands, and her new and stylish summer dress with the pleated skirt and shoes to match. Not a countrywoman's dress, certainly. Like the appointments of the house, which were of first quality and meant to last, her clothes were better suited to some matron from Foxrock or Ballsbridge, two decidedly acceptable suburbs of Dublin, than to the mistress of a rural manse. McGarr took another little nip from the flask and let the liquor seep slowly down his throat. He was beginning to feel like his old self for the first time in seventeen days.

"Fionnuala and Dan, 6th June, 1947," the caption of the wedding portrait read, and had there been some reason why that photo, which with its formal pose and sepia wash looked ancient, like a relic from some earlier age, had been pulled out for the first time in a great while? How had Fionnuala Walton—horse breeder and businesswoman—perceived time? Doubtless a busy person, had the years passed, as they had for McGarr, like coal down a chute, such that his early service on the Continent with several police forces, his return to Ireland and the Gárda, his marriage, and the more memorable cases all seemed like the day before yesterday? Had time for her too lost all its . . . reasonability? Had she become so involved in such a limited set of things that ultimately she had known herself—again like McGarr—through her work alone?

Taking yet another darling touch of "molt," as it was known in Dublin, McGarr checked his self-pitying maunderings, for indeed he was not actually in a mood to complain. So the holiday that he had looked forward to for perhaps half a year was now shot, finished, destroyed. So the wild countryside of Kildare lost in a fortnight its pleasant bloom and became a crashing bore. So horses did not suggest to him sanctuary in the transmigration of human souls. So his personal activities were rather delimited, and he had only his job, his wife, his house, his garden . . . rather, his *wife*, his job, his house, his . . . etc., he was— he now decided, taking a final, delicious belt from the pint and raising his neck to let the warmth tingle down his neck, which he swirled—very much himself, and there was an interesting containment to that.

But he had only just stoppered the flask and placed it back in his jacket when a figure appeared in the doorway and stopped to look around.

Frozen with his hand in his jacket, McGarr moved only his eyes, as the glossy, black curls that not even the tight wrap of a pony tail could keep flat swung from left to right, pausing at the two open boxes. A furrow then appeared on her brow, and she appeared to step in that direction before turning quickly toward the door which she pushed to.

Having changed out of the black dress and the flat, heelless shoes, the girl, Deirdre, now wore Wellies, bright yellow jodhpurs, and a heavy, white, woolen sweater, and over her arm was slung a cloth sack and a yellow rain slicker, as though she were about to venture out into the storm. In her other hand she held a crop and some riding gloves, which she dropped to the floor. She then hesitated and began to reach for the farrier's claw, and McGarr could not help noticing, as the sweater rode up on her back, how compact yet pleasantly full was her backside, wrapped tight in the lemon britches. A small person who was diminutive in proportions, like his own wife, Noreen, she was obviously fit. She also had that baby-fine quality of skin, which he had noted earlier, to recommend her, to say nothing of those eyes. He imagined she would feel hard/soft, a condition that would require long, patient study to plumb in all its particularity. Then, mind, she was chesty enough in her own right, and she had spirit, though McGarr wondered how much.

On the very tips of her toes, a finger on the wall for support, she had just reached the handle of the farrier's claw when suddenly she stopped and looked down. Easing herself onto her heels, she stepped back and then— was it?—gasped. McGarr thought so, and her hand came up as though to her mouth. She swung her head from left to right, then turned around as if scanning the floor or looking for something.

Outside the wind wailed in the eaves, and McGarr took the opportunity to lower his arm.

She began searching through her jodhpur pockets until her hand came up with a handkerchief. She pivoted quickly, pushing the door fully closed, and squatted down. She then reached out as though to wipe the handkerchief over the dust to expunge the print, when a footstep was heard on the landing beyond the door.

Frantic, she whipped her head toward the shadow in which McGarr was concealed, but before she could grapple up her possessions, the large, dark head of a handsome young man appeared around the top of the door.

His square face was a study in structure, the bones obvi-

21

ous and rectilinear and communicating a strength that his shoulders, swinging into the narrow, attic room, now confirmed. Like his hair, his eyes were dark and his closely shaven beard heavy, such that his skin appeared bluish in the dim light. He had a widow's peak, repeated by the line of his eyebrows, which met in the middle. In all, his appearance was heavy, ponderous, saturnine, and McGarr had seen the face before—in the wedding portrait in the trunk. "D-Deirdre, w-wha . . ." He stopped speaking, as though consciously to draw in a breath. His eyes rolled with impatience. "I-I—" The sound he then made was much like gagging. His shoulders were so heavily muscled he looked stooped.

She straightened her body but not her head. "The police. I thought you—" Her voice, though a whisper, was almost a sob. "And I—

"Close the door, for God's sake. I've to get this up."

"Wh-, wh-, wh—?" he asked, his anxiety obvious in his frustration to speak, though he complied, turning the handle carefully so the catch would make no noise. The wide fist of his other hand was clutched white by his side.

"And you know why—" she said in a passionate tone that McGarr interpreted as accusatory. "—don't tell me you don't.

"That," she pointed to the footprint in the dust. "And *that,"* to the farrier's claw. "It's enough, so it is, to see me behind bars, and I'll not have it, when . . ." Her hand came up, the one that held the handkerchief, and staunched her tears. ". . . when in all of my family and yours, she was probably the only true friend we had . . ." She bent and reached toward the dust on the floor.

"Oh!" or "No!" he cried out, and in one, powerful sweep of his arm lifted her away from the footprint. "B-been here already," he blurted out. "The p-p—"

"Police," she supplied, nodding in sudden recognition of the complexity of the situation. "You're right. Sure, they've seen it, and any change . . ." She tried to lean against him but he had turned to peer into the open trunks, after which he swung his head to her. He pointed at them.

"No, but—" She looked up at the farrier's claw, and without hesitation, it seemed, the young man—one of the Daughertys whom Stack had told him about, McGarr was willing to bet—moved right to it. Careful of the dust, he examined the implement, then turned back to her, muttering something as he reached for her things on the floor.

"Where?"

McGarr heard, "Course," or "Gorse," or "Horse."

"God, yes, and with me in such a tizzy that I can't even think straight," she said, stepping quickly to the door. There she stopped and turned back to him. "But Dan— I know your mother was to see her, then Tom and you and . . ." her pale eyes studied his dark face, ". . . but you didn't, did you?"

McGarr could not see the young man's face, but he assumed she then moved into him in a kind of embrace. After a while, she said, "Well, it's over, and there'll be some changes around here now, I'll tell you. But you're right about the horse. We must hurry. That damn Tom— do you think . . .?

Then, "Come now—we've only got 'til morning, and I'll be destroyed by then. Finished. And just when I'll need most to be on my toes, I suspect."

McGarr's thoughts exactly, though he took another small sup from the flask. Standing, he twined his fingers, turning them around as he raised his arms toward the rafters. As he stretched, he smiled to himself. Yes, the holiday—irritating as it had been—had sufficed.

Before the Technical Squad could arrive, he would conduct his own meticulous search of every drawer, closet, and dustbin in the house.

Several hours later as the short night was just ending, the two obviously older sisters of the victim were still occupying the sitting room. On a long couch, one had her head in the lap of the other, who said, "I demand to know what you're looking for?" Her own feet were propped on a hassock before a coal fire that had all but gone out.

A rag, thought McGarr. An old dress, perhaps even an old jacket or a remnant of rug. Somebody had either come equipped or taken something coarse-grained, like linen, from the attic, after having wiped it over the wall and floor.

"The person who murdered your sister, of course."

Taller and older than the victim, the woman sitting on the sofa had a heavy, fleshy face the fullness of which had long since sagged into soft, pinkish folds. Never handsome, she bore nonetheless what McGarr assumed were the family features, which seemed in her either to have been misshaped or misplaced. Her brow had too much slope, or her nose was too wide or set somewhat off to one side. In all, her face was too long or too definite. Her hair was snow white and rather poorly kept. She was wearing a tattered cardigan over an old housedress. The flesh of her swollen feet bulged from plain, black kitchen shoes that were worn and scuffed.

Her eyes—inky blue, like the victim's—met McGarr's, then moved off. "Murdered?" she asked in a small voice, glancing down at the recumbent woman, who with dark hair and lipstick and a silky, lilac-colored dressing gown patterned with silver ferns was a study in contrast. One leg was cocked to expose a shapely ankle. There were

24

matching, heelless pumps with silver pompons on her visibly veined feet. McGarr could see a line, like the edge of a mask, where her make-up ended. She did not open her eyes.

"Will there be . . . publicity?" the other asked. "The press?"

It struck him as an odd inquiry after the death of a sister with whom she had passed—could it be?—her entire life? "The business?" he asked. He then remembered what the niece and her intended had said. "Or is it the horse you're worrying about?"

She only canted her head and looked away. The corner of her left eye was very red.

McGarr considered the setting with Rosslare Harbor only a few miles distant. Deeper than Wexford Harbor, it now enjoyed the traffic of a ferry link to the Continent. People there would be used to the presence of Gárdai, customs, and other governmental officials, to say nothing of strangers. That part of Greenore Point, however, was far different, with only a few family farms—from what he could judge driving in—sharing whole square miles. He thought of the Daughertys and wondered if Stack had been able to secure an accommodation with their mother. "Not if you don't tell them."

"And your niece?" he asked, when he had completed his search of the room. "Where is she now?"

"Why?"

"I'd like to speak with her."

"Now?"

"Or later."

"In bed, I'm sure."

"Here?"

Her eyes rose to him, her nostrils flared. "I wouldn't know where else."

"Which room is hers?"

"Top of the stairs, first door on the right. I'll come with you."

"No need."

"Think you not?" she said, gently lifting the other woman's head off her lap and sliding a pillow under it.

Her step was ponderous, her heavy calves wagging with each step. She had a small goiter on the side of her neck. With the fingers of her right hand, she traced the chestnut, parquet wainscoting up to the niece's room.

"Gone," she said, after opening the door without knocking and snapping on the light.

"Where?"

"The horses, of course. There's always one or two needing something, it seems. She has her work, she does."

"Down where Dan Daugherty puts up?" The bed had not been slept in, and there were photos of horses on every wall. Saddles and tack were hanging from clotheshorses and other stands, and the room smelled strongly of leather, dubbin, and the stable.

"Her betrothed," she said, as McGarr quickly and expertly searched through the two closets and every item in the room.

"And what *is* his problem?" Opening the bedroom door wide, McGarr looked out at the foot of the stairs to the attic, which had been cordoned off with bright nylon cord hung from stainless-steel stanchions. The stairs were, say, fifteen feet from the bedroom.

"And you're—?" he asked, when after a while she had not answered.

Her deep blue eyes, agatized and depthless with age, passed quickly across McGarr's to the bedroom window. Facing east, it was filled with a storm-washed sky so clear now at daybreak that the rising sun had prickled it with points of brilliant light. Again McGarr noted the redness in the one eye.

"Siobhan. Siobhan Walton, Mr. McGarr. I run things here."

He wondered if she had been expecting him.

3

It wasn't only the voice at the door calling, "Miss Frenche, Miss Frenche—it's gone half seven now, and, like you said, I'll be puttin' your brake-fuss down," that so disoriented Noreen McGarr née Frenche, but the realization that she had suddenly awakened to the demands of a living role, as it were, and in a curious room.

Wide and long and more a kind of parlor with full bay windows than a bedroom, it had been fitted out like an apartment of a dollhouse. No surface, it seemed, remained uncluttered and everywhere—on the nightstands, the dressers, even the top of a tall armoire in one corner—lay the sort of pricey kitsch that made Noreen despair of ever making a career of her current profession, which was directing her family's picture gallery in Dublin.

Here, close to her face, was a rosy-cheeked milkmaid who had been "captured," as it were, glancing fondly over a bare shoulder at a tiny, tag-along terrier. Behind them was a *Jugendliche* in *Lederhosen* holding the hand of a breasty *Mädchen* in *Dirndl und Bluse*, and the glance they were exchanging, Noreen imagined, was enough to make any soppy heart go pit-a-pat.

But the crowning "gooey," she punned to herself—raising herself up for a better view—commanded perhaps over half of an oval table in the center of the room. Was it an ashtray? It was: of a matador plunging a gruesome saber through the chest of a charging bull. One then stubbed one's cigarette out in a depression created by a death throe in the bull's back.

Those items alone certainly Noreen could have ignored, but not—she decided, throwing back the covers and making for the toilet and shower, a good twenty-five feet away—in such number and with the consideration with which each had been selected and placed in the room. Her bath towel, hand towel, and face cloth had been staggered diagonally, like chevrons, across the back of a chair. Then, almost nothing had been chosen for function alone.

Not so the dim hallway of what even on the stormy night before had impressed Noreen as a rambling pile of a farmhouse. And she was not surprised to find its old plaster yellow and cracked and the plain, deal floor covered with scuffed lino. No doubt most other rooms but the parlor and dining room were as dourly spartan, for it was the impression of the guest rooms—duly licensed but equipped far beyond the standard of the Tourist Board—that mattered.

As with other prosperous farmers she knew, those rooms were a publicly appreciable demonstration both that the family had made it but would never themselves submit to the temptations that they could now afford. It was the puritanical—or, rather, with the Daughertys, the Jansenist—streak in the Irish character. Like reformed alcoholics who kept well-stocked bars, they themselves would only flirt but never fornicate with the illusion of plenty, which was a decadence to be enjoyed by those born to it.

For most Catholic Irish, the Famine, or at least talk of it, was still memorable. It was—she decided, moving toward the unmistakable clatter of the dining room—the great scar on the racial memory, could one credit such a concept. How else could she explain the ubiquity of "farmhouse accommodations," as they were called, with farmers who were more than simply prosperous grasping after ten easy pounds? An ineluctable peasantry?

Pausing in the doorway, she surveyed the long table that now seated seven men. Beyond a swinging door into what obviously was a kitchen, she could hear women talking as they worked. Hip-high wheat, flecked now in August with bright gamboge, had been planted as flush as a tractor would allow to a long factory window. The room itself was sunken and damp, and her line of sight was just level with the heavy spikes through which a strong wind was passing, like a capricious current through jade water. The wheat nodded. It rolled and swayed.

Well—she decided, savoring as would a diver on a cliff, the anticipation of knowing she was about to plunge herself into "character," as it were—the Irish had their strengths too: literature, music, horses, and the law, to say nothing of the stage. Then, there was a certain rough gentility that marked all diurnal concourse and upon which she could depend. It would make her mask that much easier to don, she hoped, as first one man and then another lifted his head from his plate to stare at her copper-colored curls and eyes that were greener than the wheat beyond the windows.

It was then that the swinging door bumped open. "Ah, there ya are, dear heart," said the small, rotund woman who the night before had introduced herself as Mna

30

Daugherty and had conducted Noreen to the room. Her well-muscled arms, bared by a summer dress, bore two platters heaped with country sausages and rashers. Finger waves of hair too dark to be her own color rolled out from a center part and were clutched in a bun at the back of her head. Her face was round, her nose a pert button, her mouth somewhat small. She was wearing rimless spectacles with gold bows, and her dark eyes glinted, as she took in Noreen's angular build that a thin jumper and white shorts made more emphatic.

"And I should have known, the moment I heard quiet out here in the dining room, that you'd made your entrance. Sure, wasn't I just telling the boys that I had a fancy Dublin lady for them, a looker with great, red curls and—" she swirled one of the platters and again her eyes devolved.

"And great form you're in today, if you don't mind an ould woman runnin' on. Miss Frenche, she is, boys. And Miss Frenche"—rolling quickly down the length of the table on legs that appeared too thin and bowed to support the girth of her upper body, she expertly deposited with a clump the platters on the table—"this yoke here is Tom." She shot an arm toward the ceiling to mean a handsome, graying man who sat at one end of the table. "And the devil of a fella down there with the look on him like the cutpurse who would snatch your heart, though I hear he's spoken for, is Dan Junior, named for his da.

"These others"—she meant the men in the middle of the table, who had resumed eating—"well, they'll just have to introduce themselves. I been told their names umpteen times, but every time they alight to gorge themselves at me table, they confuse themselves altogether."

All glanced up at her, dutifully smiling.

"Sure, the moment they grab up knife and fork, they

become Chow"—she pointed at one—"More Chow, Yet More Chow, Yet Again More Chow, and that pile there, lashing it in like Finn, is Chow-Chow-Chow. Chinese fellas," she laughed, craning back her head so that jowls formed on her upper chest. With a farmer's tan, freckles had appeared there and on her forehead and the knobs of her cheeks. She had a wide space between her front teeth. "Whore-ientals!"

"It's what she pays us," one chanced, when their laughter had diminished. "Coolie's wages."

"And would that you could work to deserve them," she shot back without her smile in any way diminishing.

"Now, what is it for you, this mornin', girl? Will you begin with cornflakes and juice and saunter on to a nice fry? We've also got stirabout, some lovely smoked herrings, scones, and whatever else you can see on the table. Then, God save us, I've some French coffee with chicory, and a scad of frozen croissants from Le Havre we can slap in the micro and have ready in a jiff."

She paused to gather breath, but she again surveyed Noreen, obviously liking what she saw. With her smile, her squint increased, her head turning to one side, as though listening for something only she might hear.

"But here I'm rattlin' on with you standing there, forlorn for a cuppa joe. Sit down now, get off them pins, and I'll have the girls knock up a plate for you."

Wheeling around, she snatched a towel from under her belt and slapped it on the shoulder of the man closest to her, "Push over, you lout. Git, git. There now." She passed the towel over the vacated space and stepped back. Turning, she rolled toward the swinging doors.

With a smile that, she hoped, communicated only surprise, Noreen stepped over the long bench and sat.

The man nearest her, Tom, passed his napkin across his

mouth and smiled. Like his mother's, his trunk was thick, his shoulders wide, but his hair, which had once been dark, now glinted like steel trimmings off a lathe. It made his face, which was handsome in a dark way, seem olive in tone. "She's rather much before coffee." He reached for a kettle sheathed in a quilted jacket. "It is coffee and not tea?"

Their eyes met. His were dark and warm and very clear.

Noreen nodded, and noted how perfectly his khaki shirt had been pressed. A shamrock and *Greenore Eugenics* had been stitched in green thread on the margin of a pocket. A gold chain seemed unequal to the task of containing the dark, curly hair on a wrist. Another around his neck disappeared into the coils there. He was wearing some scent—an after-shave lotion or cologne—that she could not place. Its aroma was exotic, like incense or mirrh.

"I think from all of that you caught on I'm Tom and that's Dan." He meant the dark, much younger man at the other end of the table who was also wearing a Greenore Eugenics uniform. "This is Jim." Daugherty meant the man to his left —"and Sam, Harry, Kevin, Dermot, and"— he pointed to a large, older man whose head was again within inches of his plate —"Chow-Chow-Chow," with which the company of men broke up. They roared.

The swinging door thumped open, and the mother appeared again with a plate heaped with the fry which, Noreen supposed, would be her choice for breakfast. "A great crack we're havin' here now at—" From her bodice she drew a thick gold pocket watch that was tied around her neck on a string. Expertly, with one hand she snapped it open. "Seven, bloody o'clock, God bless us."

Beside Noreen she now lowered the plate laden with

fried eggs, fried bread, fried tomatoes, rashers, and sausages choicer than those on the platter. "If I had a shtick it'd give me more pleasure than a trip to Dublin to thrash a bit of hard work out o' them slugs.

"Danny!" she shouted, raising her skirt to lift a leg over the bench to sit, facing Noreen. "What ails ye? If it's that matter you came to see me about—what's done is done, and it's not as though you'll go away from this empty-handed. Then, how's your claim the better?

"No, I understand you and what you want, and I"—she cocked her head, as though considering her choice of words carefully—"respect you for seeking it, given who you'll be there. But I'll have no," she winked at all, "greed at this table."

She then nudged Noreen and in a quiet, conspiratorial voice advised, "Oop all night, I'll bet. Con-sartin'," she winked again. " 'Tis the season.

"And then, tell me"—she asked, as all the men save her older son pulled themselves reluctantly from the table— "did you have any trouble arrivin' here last night?"

Noreen wondered if she could actually eat with the woman literally in her ear, as it were.

"On the road, just up from the harbor," she pressed.

Noreen looked up from her eggs that had been basted quickly in deep oil to lose none of their free-range flavor. "I don't understand."

"At the house, the big one there on the rise. Brick it is and lovely. A kind of mansion. It was all lit up."

Noreen paused, as if thinking. "None that I noticed, though I remember the house. Edwardian, isn't it?"

"Sure," she glanced at her son, who was finishing his coffee, "it's all that and more. You're a friend of the super's, ye say?"

Noreen hadn't, of course, but she wondered if Stack, a

34

man she knew only through the phone call she had received the night before, had. "A friend of an acquaintance," she hedged.

"And you're here for"—her head turned to her son and, Noreen suspected, an eye winked—"is it, the birds?"

It was one of Noreen's hobbies, which through Stack, her husband had suggested would afford her better cover than horsing. Then, it would only be a matter of time before somebody connected her name with the family horse farm in Dunlavin. "Yes—I'm a birder."

The admission delighted Mna Daugherty. Smiling, she moved her head to the side, as though referring the information for the consideration of some hidden jury. A characteristic gesture—Noreen suspected—it communicated either surprise at the variety of tastes in the world or a mocking pity that Noreen could be so misguided.

"Then tell us this, dear—what is it so golden you do in Dublin that midsummer finds you on the trot down here in Wexford?"

"I manage an art gallery," she said between bites.

There was a pause, then, "A *what?*"

Noreen glanced at the son, whose features remained impassive though his eyes were dancing. "An art gallery. Pictures mostly, but we also handle sculpture and sometimes silver and gold."

"Paintings, Ma," the son explained. "You know—little squares covered with colors. Then there's drawings, etchings, lithographs. Photos, gouache—" He winked at Noreen. "How's the fry?"

"Oh"—her black eyes suddenly widened—"*art!*" Reaching behind Noreen, she smacked her hand on her son's shoulder. "Wait, don't laugh. I know art, you'll see."

Snapping her head to Noreen, she demanded, "And what did you think of the room?"

Noreen swallowed a portion of fried bread that had the texture and specific gravity of a horse tablet. She knew what was expected of her, but could she bring herself to say it, *not* in the interest of art?

"Lovely," she managed. "I was taken especially by the" —she turned her head back to her plate and played the knife blade through her egg yolk—"matador."

"And the bull," said the son, laughing.

"See!" crowed the mother, "and a dead expart, she. From *Dublin*. And you, Tom, after giving out to me about the thing.

"Well, girl," she placed her hand firmly on Noreen's shoulder to help herself to a stand. "Tommy here may know a thing or two of harses, right enough, but not a dreadful lot about art.

"But I'll let you in on this—he knows the birds, and he can show you bees too, and I'll give you a tip. Beyond a handsome, well-placed man, he's also a bachelor and available and headed south over the hills this morning to Carnsore Point on a little matter of business, I'm told. By tractor, what will presarve them two little white things you call feet and make for an easy walk back.

"Meself," she said directly to the son, again removing the pocket watch from the front of her dress. "I've that matter, like we discussed, with the solicitor in Wexford, then, I suppose the registry for them foals.

"Tallyho," she said, dropping a shoulder as she turned back toward the kitchen door without one word—thought Noreen—of the murder of her nearest neighbor and the employer of her two sons, about which she undoubtedly knew. In London, perhaps, or in Paris or New York such an event could go unnoticed and undiscussed, but not in Ireland and never, like here, in what Noreen thought of as *deep* country.

Decorum, she wondered? A concern for propriety or the feelings of the family of the deceased? Or perhaps the discretion of the perfect hostess?

Noreen rather doubted it. If Mna Daugherty did not gossip, Noreen McGarr née Frenche would gladly eat another slice of fried bread.

Yet riding the universal chuck of the tractor and holding onto its seat, a heavy woolen jumper tied round her waist and her binoculars strapped over a shoulder, Noreen soon forgot the matter that had brought her to the five-by-ten-mile block of rolling farmland and broad, sandy beaches—some extending at low tide for miles into St. George's Channel—that was known as the "cornerstone of Ireland."

It was the sunniest and one of the warmest spots in the country, and under a strong summer sun its beaches were thronged with bathers, the margins of its fields dotted with caravans and tents. Byways down to the shore were clogged with cars, yet twenty feet to any side the quiet, "business" of the year-round residents continued apace.

To be heard over the clatter of the diesel tractor, she had to lean in close to Daugherty and shout, asking him why it was that one side of the simple farm road was in pasture, while the other was planted every square inch with grain?

Turning so that—it seemed to her—their bodies would more than simply touch and he could speak into her ear, he asked, "You want it simple or with the frills?"

She smiled and averted her head, ostensibly to watch the flight of a pair of corn buntings, startled from a hedge. "Here I am, searching for simplicity, only to discover a complicated man who is about to tell me this is complicated country. Frankly, sir, I'll refuse to believe it."

37

At her playful tone, Daugherty's smile grew more complete, his eyes moving over her lips.

"And mind the way, while you propound this fiction." She pointed to a fence, into which they were about to crash, then reached for the wheel, which together they wrenched clear of the hazard, though she suspected the maneuver devised.

Through a broad smile, he said, "On the simplest level, there are three kinds of soil from Rosslare Harbor to Carnsore Point. "There's a small amount of poorly drained land, best for pasture, where the Waltons put the house. Then a broad stretch of maybe the finest corn-growing land in all of Ireland." He nodded once, as though to stress the significance of that statement; by corn he meant wheat. "Given our average one hundred and fifty-two days of sun here and prevailing breezes from the southwest, the growing season can stretch from January to November.

"Finally, there's an acceptable though sandy soil beginning at Churchtown, the little village up ahead, and stretching to Carnsore Point.

"For your purposes"—he again swung his head to her and made sure their eyes met—"birding?"

"Why else should I be in your company?" she answered.

He laughed and turned back to the tarred road to the village that they were now approaching. "It means in the wet land that the hedges 'll be mainly willow with some gorse, alder, hawthorn, elm, and birch. On the good land —hawthorn, ash, and blackthorn grow powerfully well, with a small amount of early gorse. Willows you'll seldom see here, but once in a while ash, elm, oak, sycamore, and even pine.

"Past the town here"—they were nearly upon it, and cars filled with vacationers swung by them at speed on the narrow and now macadam road—"the hedges decline dramatically in height and quality, you'll see. There's gorse with bracken, some holly with birch, mountain ash, and broom. Oaks are the main tree species, though you'll see others planted, with all that might mean for your birds."

"Which is?" Noreen was rather surprised at his specific knowledge of the land hereabouts. True, he had been raised on a farm and now worked here, but she could think of few other country people of her acquaintance who could expatiate with such particularity on the species of wild growth in their areas.

"You're asking me?"

Said she, "If I were planning my guide right now, I'd write, 'Apart from dreadful flirts, the natives hereabouts fancy gold' "—she plucked the chain around his neck— "and watch that car! Janie, we're kilt!"

Daugherty stopped the tractor, and a large sedan, packed with children and a distracted driver, bore down on them. At the last moment, it swerved and roared past, though Daugherty only kept his eyes—dark and winning —on Noreen.

" 'But of the birds,' " she continued, somewhat flustered under his stare, " 'they know nothing.' And no, Mr. Daugherty, I do not want a drink."

In a small, dark bar, cooled by thick stone walls and a stone floor, Daugherty placed two half pints of chilled lager on the table and sat rather too close to her on a padded wall seat that allowed them to survey the pub entire.

Said he, "Along the shore you might see great-crested grebes, shovelers, the common scoter, kingfisher, roseate tern, and little tern. In the fields, corn bunting, stock dove, and black cap. Also barn owl, if you dare to venture out at night." He raised his glass and waited until Noreen touched hers to it.

"Then on the heath or the scrubland south of here you'll find nightjar, stonechat, and grasshopper warbler, though you'd have better sense to look for the snow that fell last winter than to see them all at one go.

"And sure—" he again made certain his eyes locked into hers, and she felt a little thrill that she credited to flattery. He reached down and lifted her left hand from which fortunately she had stripped her rings, though were he to look closely he might see the mark left by her wedding band. "—if you bided here the while and marked down all I said for the guide, who'd be the bit the wiser? Then we could go someplace quiet like, and I could repeat it all slow for true."

The barman's eyes met Noreen's in the mirror in back of the bar. "With elaborations, of course?" she asked.

"Oh, at your suggestion," he chuckled, his tanned face suddenly lined with quiet mirth.

"And I would," she said, placing his hand back on the khaki of his thigh, "though if that's the simple explanation as to why the eastern fields are pasture and the western crop, I confess I'm more than ready to hear the complex."

"Fair play and easily done," he replied affably. "The crops side—corn, oats, barley with some potatoes, sugar beets, and apple orchard, and about fifty other acres of rutabagas and other fodder roots—that's ours. The pastures? Theirs."

"Whose?"

His eyes moved off toward the barman and then a couple that had just entered. He turned back to her, and in a low voice said, "The Waltons'."

"On Greenore Point?"

He blinked, "You know them?"

"Only the mailbox and the house. It's the one your mother asked me about, is it not? With all the lights it looked like a party. I thought at first it was your house."

"Us? A *party*? Ah, no—as you might have guessed, having met my mother, we're simpler people than that."

"But don't you work for them?"

"Who?"

"The Waltons." She reached over and ran a finger across the stitching on the margin of the pocket of his khaki shirt. It read "Greenore Eugenics" in intricate, Gaelic script. The buttons were also green and shaped like shamrocks.

"You read that on their mailbox as well?" His smile had fallen somewhat.

"No, actually—" she glanced up at the barman, who was conversing with some other employee and glancing her way. In a panic she asked herself where near the Walton house she had seen the shamrock logo and name. "—it was on a . . . fence," she remembered. The headlamps of her mother's car, which she had borrowed, had picked it out, as she had rounded a corner. "I believe."

"You're observant and have brilliant eyes. Those little signs—one every half mile—can't be more than two inches high."

"And you're evasive," she countered. "What's your capacity—there."

"I'm director." He drained the glass and set it down on the table. "Just. I was promoted from manager the other day."

"Then you're not a farmer."

"You don't fancy farmers?"

"Horses are so much more . . . agreeable than crops, wouldn't you say?"

"Then how do you feel about eugenics?" he asked.

"I should imagine with my body, when it moves me."

Daugherty smiled and stood. Noreen wondered how old he could be. Forty at most, his years in the sun and wind having imparted a leathery quality to his skin that both denied any suggestion of youth and made him appear ageless. Having noted the aging process in active outdoorsmen, such as he, of her father's generation, she imagined that he would remain hale-looking and handsome until the decline just before death.

Twenty minutes later when they had reached the base of Carnsore Point, Daugherty gallantly jumped down off the tractor to help her from the chuck.

"Is this really necessary, sir?" she asked. The drop was perhaps three feet.

"Absolutely. I hope you don't think I'd drive you all the way out to this lonely spot and let you hop off on your own."

And when Noreen extended her arms and leaned toward him, he cried, "Oh, look—a puffin!" She glanced up in the direction of his gaze, and he drew her body down on him, his face grazing her neck and sending a chill through her that caused her to turn her head to the side. She smelled his scent or perfume or whatever it was. He tried to kiss her, but she moved her head away. "Tonight?" he asked.

"That's not a complete thought," she said, stepping back from him but flushed nonetheless. And she put the feeling of excitement down to a mere, momentary, physical attraction. He was, after all, an attractive and strong man who was younger than her husband. Certainly he was more fit, and then he and she had horses and the country and banter in common. When, she asked herself, had she and her husband last had a playful conversation together, to say nothing of a flirt?

"Me and you. Tonight. I'll take you to dinner at the hotel in Wexford, then on to the grandest party to be seen in these parts in centuries. I have a Greek friend with a great, garish barge of a boat." He reached for her wrist, but she held up a palm.

"Impetuous as well as evasive, is it, Mr. Daugherty?" She asked herself if she were feeling what her friends had described to her when they confided about their "flings" —doubly hot, knowing it was wrong. The one who had insisted Noreen give it a try had taken a holiday alone in Provence where she had met not one but several men. Far from sleazy, she had made her visit seem both romantic and enticingly self-indulgent. Then, Noreen had done little without at least her husband's knowledge for nearly a decade. Sometimes she felt as though she had been a mere child when she married and had never granted herself the chance of acting on her own.

"You're brilliant. A rose."

And when was the last time her husband had professed his affection? She could not remember, and hoped it wasn't just his age. Some other friends, even her mother, had warned her against marrying a man so much older than she. "The difference isn't distinct now, but it will be as years go by. I've seen it with couples right here in Dunlavin," whom she then named. Her mother.

Then she had said, "It would be one thing were he a sportsman, but, my dear, consider his occupation and habits." At the time Noreen had considered the comment a mere elaboration of prejudice.

"Hyperbole will get you everywhere, but you've obviously learned that from experience," she now answered, turning from Daugherty to begin her ascent of the point. Or was it just the glorious day and the fact that she had stepped into a role outside of herself in a new and different setting, courtesy of her husband, she reminded herself? "We'll see how you feel about all this later."

"Then that isn't a no, which I would in any case refuse to accept," he shouted at her back.

"Nor is it a yes, and you'll take what you're given."

Under a hot, summer sun the headland of reddish rock rose like a megalith before her. Gulls, disturbed by her presence, peeled off the edge of the path and on updrafts hovered in place until she had passed by.

Turning herself into the cooling breeze, Noreen looked west over a stretch of spectacular sand dunes and sandy tidal spits which, but for water on two sides, comprised a kind of desert. To the south was St. George's Channel with the tan-colored cliffs of the Saltee Islands in the distance. To the north were paler waters—today from the promontory of Carnsore Point a vivid ultramarine—that were the coastal lagoons of Lady's Island Lake, Tacumshin Lake, and Ballyteige Lough where the spits had impounded streams draining nearby hills. And the view was so altogether different from any other in Ireland that Noreen decided to sit on a flat shelf of granite and drink in full measure of sand, sea, and sun.

It was a glorious day, she decided, with high, ballooning clouds, like chains of dreams, coasting in lofty puffs northwest toward England. The wind—raking the channel from the direction in which Daugherty had gone—roared in her ears, but strangely she suddenly could no longer hear the tractor.

Standing, she touched the binoculars to the bridge of her nose and trained her sight down the line of the dunes from which the wind was now lifting long, sparkling tails of buff sand. But nothing. Not a sign of him.

Even when—asking herself what she would do or say if

he discovered her following him—she found where the tractor had left the field, she could not see him anywhere: toward the lighter water of Little Lady Lake to the west or back to the north in the mostly open fields the way they had come. There was not one moving object between her and the church, which evidently had given that town its name.

Lowering the binoculars, she turned and heeled herself down a sandy declivity toward the dune behind which, she thought she remembered, the tractor had vanished. But in the wind its track had disappeared, and the sand, spraying up into her face, made her lose her bearing. Then, everything looked so similar, now that she was down among the dunes. The tractor must have climbed back up into a pasture, she concluded, though she could see no point at which that would have been possible.

Yet she trudged on toward the water, the hard sand fringe of which she would follow to Greenore Point. And now without even the company of the role she had devised for herself.

After all, it was such a splendid day. Pity her husband —or at least somebody—wasn't there to share it with her, she thought.

4

McGarr had no such need. Most of his night and all of his day had been filled with the usual details of what was now an official investigation with one salient exception: no press and he wondered why.

Granted, the Walton house was somewhat isolated, set off on the bald landscape about a half mile from the Greenore lighthouse. And then apart from himself and Stack and the men from the Technical Squad, only the victim's sisters, Siobhan and Machala, and the niece, Deirdre, and her intended, Dan Daugherty, Jr., knew of the murder. But in all rural Irish settings that McGarr had previously known, gossip (to say nothing of gossip of a death) enjoyed at least some currency, and though it was refreshing not to have the Fourth Estate underfoot, it made him wonder why the news had not gotten out.

True, there were no servants, and when McGarr—perhaps himself the cause—had suggested that Stack wait until the press contacted him and then refer the matter to Dublin Castle, the Rosslare superintendent had replied, "Those louts? I wouldn't give them the time of day." And later, after McGarr's admonition concerning the presence of his wife, "Sure, you only have to tell me onc't."

But certainly young Daugherty knew, and by the account of Siobhan, the elder of the surviving Walton sisters —McGarr now turned his head from the sitting room window to watch her settle her tall ungainly body again in the sofa; she smoothed a kitchen apron over another worn housedress—he lived away from Greenore House. Wasn't the news of a neighbor and an employer's death worth repeating, could he so manage? Wouldn't he even have told, say, his mother, bad terms or no? Wouldn't she then have phoned other interested parties until finally the story reached the ears of those who were paid to spade over misfortune?

Siobhan's hands were red and appeared swollen from washing up. The sclera of her left eye was understandably more bloodshot after what little sleep she could have got since.

Then, Greenore Eugenics certainly had commerce with the outside world, though when McGarr, interested in who would answer the phone, had rung the number, nobody had answered. But without a doubt clients, owners, other breeders, purveyors, perhaps the local vet—all those people whom he had kept seeing at his father-in-law's gate—would in the normal course of things communicate with the facility. Had they not been told? Would they not be informed at least of some managerial change at the top?

Conclusion? For some reason, nobody had been told by at the very least four of the people who had been closest to the victim, and McGarr wanted to know why. Privacy? Unconcern? Perhaps some matter as banal as an impending horse sale or as central as the settlement of an estate which was obviously of no small value? Who were these people?

He glanced at Machala, who was smaller and thinner than Siobhan, with hair the very color of the victim's but brushed back slick at the sides to make more stylishly emphatic the steely mane that now flowed over the back of the sofa. Hers was a face that would have been oval, if not for cheekbones that were prominent and set rather close to her eyes. They were the same deep blue and focused on a point near the ceiling at which, from time to time, she directed the smoke from a cigarette. With a definite jaw and a thinly bridged nose, her appearance was indeed severe.

She was sitting slumped down in the sofa and wearing —again like the victim—some costly and stylish blouse with padded shoulders and a front placket which, given her position, had opened to expose a glimpse of her chest. The skin there was smooth and firm, the globe of a breast a milky white as though she had been sunbathing in a skimpy costume.

How old could she be—McGarr wondered—if at sixty-two her dead sister had been the youngest? Her well-tanned legs were crossed and exposed to mid-thigh by a center-front slit that extended deep into the skirt. On her feet were new, black and shiny pumps, the leather soles of which had never been worn beyond the soft carpets and polished floors of the house.

McGarr assumed the seat across from them, and from a vinyl evidence case drew out two objects which he placed on the coffee table between them. "Ladies—enlighten me."

Again it was the elder sister, Siobhan, who spoke first. "That's Fionnuala, of course, in the full bloom of her womanhood—with Dan. The picture was taken, as was the custom then, in the photographer's studio in Wexford, a day or two before they were to be married.

"And would you look at her—" Siobhan leaned forward and with a work-reddened hand picked up the portrait, which she held so that both could examine it. It was only then McGarr noticed that her sister had taken her other hand. "—that worried look, in spite of the blush, as if, even then, she knew she'd soon sup sorrow.

"Because of that—" Siobhan flicked her chin at the bottomless green bottle which had been found in the dead woman's hands. It was the second item on the table; in the briefcase McGarr had a third. "—or, rather, because of Dan."

"Daugherty?" McGarr asked.

"The same. The father, though in spite of the stutter the son is his image and not just in form.

"You see, Fionnuala had been sheltered and—" The old woman turned her head to the bank of three French doors which opened on a terrace; beyond was a pasture, a hedge, and then much in the distance a beach and the sea.

Somewhere close by a horse was whinnying.

"—spoiled, and, like always, it only made her soft and unable to suffer scorn, as we all must. Being the youngest and"—her head moved slightly to the sister beside her—"prettiest, she got everything from our father who doted on her."

The sister, Machala, turned her head and looked down at the parquet floor that was covered by a thick woolen rug in some russet color. A single tear clung to a wrinkle that McGarr had not previously seen beneath her chin. In the hearth a fresh coal fire was burning in spite of the day.

"When she was still only a child, he bought her horses not ponies, hired in tutors not nannies. London, Paris—he took her everywhere, though to be truthful she only deserved the attention and blossomed under it. Brilliant, she was, in everything but particularly science and mat's. And it delighted Daddy who was, you know, an engineer and the man who designed the Glasgow Flyer." It was a railroad engine about which McGarr, who had lived in Inchicore near Dublin's Heuston Station, had heard talk of as a youth; it had been fast and reliable and capable of pulling great loads.

"My first remembrance of them together was of her standing over there by those windows, totting up figures —smiling like, her head cocked to one side, pulling the sums right out of the air like they were something only she could see. Smashin'. She couldn't have pleased Daddy more if she had won the Grand National.

"But thorns are sown and grown, and he sent her off first to Trinity and then Cambridge, with everything she could possibly want, even a motorcar and a *servant* or two.

"Then it was the biology she studied, but not like other women of the brainy type for doctoring, which wasn't enough for her. No. Genetics, she would pursue there at university in England. It would be her career, though it wasn't, as she imagined, to be."

Horses had appeared in the pasture beyond the terrace, and Siobhan turned her eyes to them.

"At Daddy's insistence she came home that summer. He wasn't feeling well, though he never complained, and he must have known his time was short."

Now Machala's face, which she had turned away toward the wall, was streaming with tears that were dropping regularly onto the satiny surface of her blouse. The two sisters' hands were still clasped.

"Well, sir, it was then that Dan Daugherty came home from the British war where he—the only man from these parts, mind—had gone to 'get blooded,' some said. But" —she cocked her head—"he was tall and dreadful handsome and fit and tanned and now . . . worldly, if you understand the way of soldiers. Death on the one hand," her eyes flickered toward her sister, "and something new —another field or town or country—on the other." Her gaze returned to the windows.

As she spoke, all else in her face seemed to move save the heavy pocket of goiter in her neck. She was wearing the same dress McGarr had seen her in the night before. On her feet were the black, battered houseshoes, and McGarr wondered what exactly her position in the household was and why she had emphasized the word servant? Certainly Greenore House did not lack for care. Did Machala pitch in? Or the niece? And then, which one of them and by how much would gain from the death?

"Full of tales, he was—France, Greece, Turkey. Knowing horses and all, he was put in what was left of the real horse cavalry, and later sent out to the Middle East as a kind of expert on breeding. They had, of course, a good bit of their own horses, but they admired the English thoroughbred, and Dan went there to help them improve what of those horses they had.

"Wild as the west wind, he was, and, wouldn't you have guessed, a poet. There in them foreign parts, he grew a bit homesick, I think—though he would have been the last to admit it—he'd written a book of poems. And he wasn't home a few months before he had it out. *Tuskar Rock and Other Poems.* In the *Times* Butler Yeats called it," she closed her eyes, " 'a voyage on those currents between speech and silence where one discovers discrete

51

images artfully evoked,' but beyond that notice and the one sentence of praise hardly anything more. It was slighter, I believe, than he had hoped.

"But"—Siobhan sighed—"he had other things on his mind by then—his own small holding, which his father had left him, and Daddy"—she paused and shook her head—"had hired him on as our . . . steward or gillie or 'manager.' He was ill, our daddy." She turned her head to her sister, who did not respond.

"To his credit, though, Dan had his talents and was probably too good a farmer. A natural. Like in his poems, he had an abiding feel for the land and this part of Wexford.

"And when Fionnuala came home, done in from her studies and all the professors so different from Dan, it was only a matter of days before she was desperate over the man. Not eating. Dressing herself to kill. Lighting up like a filament whenever he was around.

"Then, ag'in to give the divil his due, Dan was capable —too capable, you'll see—and sure of himself and life and"—she cast her free hand toward the doors—"the promise that the sun would shine on him and his for all of his days and, you know." Siobhan swung her head to McGarr, and for the first time since she had begun speaking their eyes met, "he wasn't far wrong, though by then Fionnuala loved him in her heart's core and there was no rectifying that.

"Daddy, looking out from his sick bed and seeing her riding a tractor with him, having to hold on so like a cockle to a rock, tried to send her away. But bold now— the legacy, like I said, of his sufferance—she refused. The harvest came. Then autumn and her studies, which she told us she wouldn't—she *couldn't*—return to. 'I've found a place,' she announced one morning at breakfast after having bided the night with him, I was sure, 'here in the country.'

" 'And what will you do, dear, here in the country?' asked Daddy.

" 'Raise horses,' says she, 'like you.'

"There was a pause that lasted, I think, t'irty seconds but seemed a lifetime, and I can hear it still. It was the silence that sealed all our fates. Sure, after his death Machala and I would have probably otherwise followed Fionnuala to England and London. There was nothing really for us here. Daddy had been a patriot himself. Hadn't he given us Irish names and fought for independence in the Revolution itself?

"But the country had changed and was changing still more and not to our liking. And we were still young and had . . . prospects, had we only known so then."

Machala's body quaked. She raised her other hand and bit a knuckle.

"Daddy only shook his head and looked away, as much as to say, the waste, the terrible waste. All her talent and beauty, all the time and money lavished on one who would become no more than a farmer's wife, though not even that was to be and—when all was said and done—it turned out he had undervalued Fionnuala's brains and spunk.

"By Christmas she'd gotten Dan to propose, by Easter the banns were being read at St. Malachi's." Siobhan glanced at McGarr and raised an eyebrow. "That's right, the Roman Church. It was a concession our family, which has been here since the fourteenth century, mind, had never made, and for his mother, who was a biddy and a gossip and, as it turned out, an uncharitable woman.

"Says Fionnuala, 'It's merely a formality and means nothing to me. A way of appeasing the local deities, so to speak. The country is Catholic, and should I choose to cast my children pariahs?' Like she was directing a play or a . . . genetics laboratory.

"It's that, I think, that she ran afoul of in the long run —seeing things always in her own eyes and her eyes alone, for all her education which was—mind you—science. Strictly science."

Had McGarr heard a half note of pride? He had, and he wondered at Siobhan's background and Machala's. There seemed such a disjunction between the way the former spoke and the latter dressed. Dublin, London, New York—McGarr imagined that Machala could blend into the more fashionable sections of any of those cities, whereas Siobhan's life, from the look of it, had been nothing but tea, cows, and gossip. And there they sat holding hands.

"For through the Daughertys' eyes—and I blame that grasping shrew of a mother—the marriage could not have made better sense," Siobhan continued. "Their property then was encircled by ours, with access to the main road and the harbor and even to the beaches for the kelp that they still used for fertilizers *by permission only*, mind. Years gone by, you see, they had been debtor tenants, allowed to remain at the forbearance of our great-great-great grandfather alone. When he died, he willed them those forty acres and the house, which remained for generations an unsightly smirch midst our holdings. A common dirt farm, here on land that had raised Derby winners in 1902 and 1905.

"The marriage, though, would have ended that, and, sure, Dan was a horseman himself. County jumping champ, whenever he had time to enter the test. Like I said, he had the knack and luck. Anything he touched his hand to.

"Until"—she flicked out her free hand at the two objects on the coffee table and her eyes seemed suddenly glassy with compassion—"the 'blowing' began a week, maybe two before the wedding. Night after night. Unabated until the early hours of the morning. Nobody could sleep, and Daddy kept phoning the Guards." She blinked. "They came and it stopped, but whoever it was would only return, after they'd left.

"Who—we asked ourselves—had we offended, and how? Hadn't we even relented on the question of religion? How could anybody see the marriage as anything but a victory for the Irish?" Her eyes met McGarr's and moved off. "Fionnuala herself? Had she, whose heart would neither stain nor spot in her love of that man, done something blameworthy? But even then," she nodded her head once, "we should have known the author of our misery, though he professed ignorance of the cause.

"And the wailing, the crying from the hedges, the hills, as though from some poor, dying, defenseless thing was so desperate and pitiable in its sound that Daddy said it would kill him sure, could he not make it stop. Three days before the wedding he raised himself from his bed, mounted his horse, and began asking round.

"He was a kindly man and had earned friends and was taken aside and told the truth—that Fionnuala's marriage to Dan Daugherty could never be, since Dan was known to be the father of the child Mna Doran would soon birth. It would have been one thing had she been a *jolly* type with a . . . following, if y' ken me meaning. But she was then just sixteen years old and had been 'tutored' by Dan and was the only daughter of canny farmers who we—as the story goes—had evicted from their ancient seat here on Greenore Point.

"Fionnuala said she didn't care, that she scorned their

peasant morality, that Dan could have 'covered'—her very words, like she was speaking of a stud—every filly in the county, for all she cared. Dan was her betrothed and they would marry.

"But a question of money or land or legality—well, that was something for debate in a court of law, but the view on morality and, more, *paternity*, then was very strict in these parts. The people who were blowing had decided all that for themselves, and Daddy could only concur. He returned to his bed and never rose from it again.

"But still she fought it, Fionnuala—going to Dan and saying she didn't care, that they'd move. England. Australia, the States. They'd make out. But—again—she was seeing it all through her own eyes, and Dan, to do him justice, was not one to cut and run. He—not she—called the marriage off. He would do the 'right' thing by Mna and the Dorans, if not by Fionnuala.

"The 'blowing' of course, stopped, and Fionnuala was destroyed utterly for a while. Daddy's death followed soon after, which only made matters worse for us but especially for Fionnuala, believing, as she did, that she had killed him."

Machala's body twitched again; her face was streaming with silent tears.

"But just to show you how well-suited they were to each other, Fionnuala did not pack up and leave either, as all had expected. Saying to us at least that she did not need the hand if she had the heart, she plunged into the farm here, as if they had in fact been married and were working it together. With the new wife and baby and failing mother and poor farm, you see, Dan needed whatever work he could get, and—harken while I whisper this—they were a *natural* couple, those two." Her eyes, one bloodshot, widened emphatically. "Him the practical side of things and her the t'eoretic.

"The breeding business had been their goal when engaged and it became their mutual project after his marriage. They took some of the ideas each possessed, and with Machala here handling the books it wasn't long before Greenore Eugenics, as she called us (again to be different from the common stud farm), soon prospered like few other such consarns here in Ireland.

"As well, with the business of his own small holding, which Fionnuala helped him add to and improve whenever and wherever she could, and all the work breeding, birthing, weaning, raising, selling, and whatnot here, wasn't she with him more than the wife herself and without the . . . domesticity, which was something she admitted to me she abhorred. She leased him the acres that—because she would not, like Daddy, risk grazing the horses exclusively—we no longer needed, and under contract he tilled the fields and grew the grain that the stables required."

Obviously tired, Siobhan reached up with her free hand and depressed the lid of the bloodshot eye. "And everything went swimmingly until Dan died."

"When was that?"

"A year and three—no—four months ago."

"What happened then?"

From Rosslare Harbor came the bellow of an ocean ferry. "Machala can tell you more than me, but Fionnuala promoted Tom, the first son, who knows horses and deserved it. Made him director, as his father had been before him. But she terminated Binn na Rinn Farms as Greenore Eugenics' supplier of record, and put Mna Daugherty on notice that she would not renew the option Dan had taken on the land we no longer needed for pasture. It was that, as I said, that Mna had been 'renting,' which is not even the proper word, private like. Fionnuala said she would put those parcels and"—she shook her head—"much of what you can see that's open farm fields from here to Carnsore Point up for auction with all that meant in terms of development. Speculators in land and building tracts and the type of men who slap up vacation cottages and such truck swarmed all over the Eugenics the moment word got out she was even considering selling the property."

"What acreage are we speaking of?"

"That the Daughertys rented?"

McGarr nodded.

"Four hundred and eighty acres all told."

In any part of Ireland a sizable tract, but especially there where the land was rich and the climate warm and sunny.

He turned to Machala so she would know he was addressing her. "And your opinion?" When she did not answer, he said, "I say, I'd like your opinion."

Slowly the woman turned a face that seemed like it was dissolving in tears. Her head was quaking. "Of what?" In the light from the pasture her deep blue eyes seemed almost green. There was a smudge, like a graying wash of watercolors, where her eye shadow had gathered on the side of her chin.

"Of . . . all this." McGarr's hand swept out to mean the blower, the wedding portrait, and what Siobhan had said.

"Why?"

"Because I must know."

"Why *must* you?"

"Because—as Siobhan here seems to realize, your sister was murdered."

"By whom?"

McGarr glanced at Siobhan for any reaction, but she only held her gaze out the French windows. "I'll soon know," he said.

Machala shook her head. "I don't believe it. Nothing of what you say or Siobhan either. Not a word of it. Fionnuala was a domineering bitch, and only in death did Dan Daugherty escape her. She tried—and the horrible part is she didn't care how she *succeeded*—to control everybody and everything, even natural processes. In that, as in all else, she was utterly ruthless, and if she was murdered, then"—she let out a little cry and cast her eyes, which had again begun to flood with tears, toward the ceiling—"there's a place in heaven for whoever had the courage to do her in."

"Any ideas?" McGarr tried not to stare. Now in addition to their appearances, their opinions of the victim conflicted, yet their hands remained firmly clasped.

"Fionnuala had dressed for Mna Daugherty, who had an appointment to see her at half three. Her son Dan Junior had then arranged to see Fionnuala immediately after."

"About what?"

"Sure the only three things that would move Mna Daugherty to stray from her house and come here: money, land, or her sons—in that order. In this case it was all three and *Deirdre* and Dan Junior."

"What about them?"

"You could ask them or her."

"I will, I will that, but I'm asking you."

Her left hand came up to her brow, and in a tired voice she said, "What else but to maintain the privileges, the . . . hegemony that the Daughertys have asserted over Walton holdings since Fionnuala decided she would bind

Dan to her as totally as if they actually *had* been married. Him bringing to her little arrangement his best hours, his best efforts, his talents, and she her brains, her love for him, and our property. Mna Daugherty now misses the convenience and the . . ."

"Profit," supplied Siobhan.

Machala nodded. "And that most grievously I'm sure. Then where, hereabouts, could she find so much good, dry land so . . ."

"Cheap," said her sister.

She nodded, "And so convenient."

As though the interview were now nearly through, McGarr moved up to the edge of the seat and placed the blower and wedding portrait back in the vinyl case. He took his time, maneuvering the objects down away from the third thing he had carried in. It had been his experience to note that at the end of a long interview, people suddenly dropped their guard, and he made it a point to save at least one vital question until last.

"Why is it," he chanced, standing, "that your father left his estate to his youngest daughter?"

Said Machala, "Well—she was about to get married, wasn't she? I don't know if it was the fact that she didn't that killed him. But Dan Daugherty's making a fool of her —*us*—before the entire county couldn't have helped. But having no brothers . . ." Her voice trailed off, and she looked away.

"And now?" McGarr asked. "Which of you now will inherit from Fionnuala?"

Said Siobhan, "For all her intelligence Fionnuala was flighty and who's to tell? But, sure, for a woman my age, where's the difference? I have a place in this house. She won't have denied me that. Or Machala, either, after all our service here.

"Deirdre, perhaps, though we won't know for certain before the will is read."

"Why Deirdre?"

Machala snapped, "She has a future, hasn't she?"

Said McGarr, "With Dan Daugherty." He waited, watching them closely, his hand still in the vinyl case.

And when neither replied, he pulled out and, like an amulet before two specters, held up the farrier's claw. "What's this?" he demanded.

A Technical Squad examination had revealed that an attempt had been made to wipe it clean, though the shaft now bore a woman's fingerprints—the thumb and index finger of the right hand. Machala looked away, her fist again coming up to her chin.

Said Siobhan, "It's one of Dan's tools, the ones he used while in the army. A farrier, he was for a time. Sergeant," she added with no little pride. "Fionnuala hung them up in the attic"—only then did her eyes rise to McGarr— "after Dan died. Is that what—?"

McGarr cocked his head, his eyes remaining firmly on her. "What *what?*"

She only shook her head and pulled her eyes away, as though distressed.

"A year and four months ago, Dan's death?" McGarr pressed.

She nodded, "Everything about Dan was sacred for her. After his death she as much as enshrined him.

"The wife? After the funeral she went straight to her solicitor and signed on some property she optioned with the death benefit from an assurance policy. The greengrocer came next. And then the butcher. Finally a wee drink in a pub. The barman stood the round, out of respect for the dead."

What was it McGarr was hearing? Gossip? He rather

thought so, and it piqued his interest.

"Yesterday your sister took her dinner here at Greenore House?" he asked, appropriating the term used in the country to mean the midday meal.

Siobhan nodded.

"You were here as well?"

Machala nodded too.

"And your sister—what did she do after her dinner?"

"She went upstairs to prepare for her 'appointment.' Her words." Machala's jaw was now rigid, and her eyes moved to the farrier's claw.

"With Mna Daugherty?"

"And afterward, the son."

"Which one?"

"Dan."

"Why?"

"To present his side of the case, though he needn't have."

"Case?"

"For their marriage. Deirdre and Dan, though with Deirdre present at dinner she didn't say."

"But what exactly?" McGarr insisted.

The sisters swapped glances, then looked away.

"After dinner, then—what did she do? Fionnuala."

Machala withered him with her gaze.

"And you—what did you do?"

She blinked, "Is this an interrogation, as its called?" McGarr kept staring, until she added, "I went back to my work of course, as I was expected."

"What time was that?"

"Half one."

"And Deirdre?"

Said Siobhan, "She went upstairs for her nap. She's never been strong."

McGarr thought of her diminutive but square body and the taut muscles straining under the material of her riding trousers.

"And you?"

"Wash-up," said Siobhan perfunctorily. "I went into the kitchen and me work."

A note of resentment? McGarr could not tell.

"And you didn't hear your sister fall?"

Both women stared hard at him, before Siobhan shook her head.

"But Deirdre heard her?"

Said Machala, "After her nap, Deirdre went down to the stables for Dan. He'd already left for here for his . . . turn at Fionnuala's ear, so she said. Across the fields and not by the road.

"Not finding him, she went into Kilranell on an errand. It was when she returned that she found her."

"All that by car?"

Machala nodded. "The Morris Minor. The old one. All beat up." Her own was a Jaguar XK 140, an antique of sorts but kept in splendid repair with a vanity plate that read "Mach W." McGarr had noticed it parked round the side of the house and had checked its registration.

"Deirdre told you that?

"She told both of us that. You don't, I hope, think we would not have discussed our own sister's death?"

Not in Ireland, McGarr thought, glancing out at the pasture and feeling suddenly tired.

"Whose errand?"

"Mine," said Siobhan. "I needed twenty pounds of praties, half a block of white cheese, a kilo of coffee, and some prawns. Healy's, she shopped in. I've the receipt in the kitchen."

"Where you entertained Tom Daugherty that afternoon—for how long?"

"Until he tired of waiting and had to go back to work."

"And he did that."

"Directly. Didn't I watch him from the window over the sink, passing across the fields toward the stables?"

McGarr placed the farrier's claw back in the vinyl case, which he closed. "You should mind that eye," he said. "A blood vessel's broken, and it could lead to complications."

She glanced toward the French window and the field beyond.

"It's nothing. Eye strain."

"No glasses?"

She shrugged. "They're little help."

The fingerprints were Deirdre's, McGarr was almost sure. He had found their match in the niece's room.

He would speak with her, he would. After he made a few phone calls in Kilranell.

Then, McGarr did not have to look to know his flask was empty.

5

Having climbed up through beach rubble and along a narrow path about an hour later, Noreen found her way into the fields south of Greenore Point blocked by a ditch, a tightly chinked stone wall, and a brambly hedge. An oxer, she thought, the hot breeze over the wall carrying to her both the trumpeting of a stallion and the moist funk of stables.

At length she found a stile, but when she stepped carefully up the granite slabs and turned at the top of the wall, she was surprised by what she saw. Instead of the pleasant bucolic scene of gently rolling fields bordered by hedgerows and dotted with small, thatched or slate-roofed cottages, she was presented with a vast open pasture shaped like a five-sided shell. On the middle plain was grouped a complex of buildings that more closely resembled a modern factory than a farm.

All were new or at least modern in design and, unlike Greenore House, built for function, not show. The stables were towering Nissen huts, the aluminum roofs shimmering like quicksilver in the midday summer sun and so bright that Noreen could not look at the four or—were there five?—of them directly. With bay doors open front and rear to catch the breeze, they looked like aircraft hangars or great steel tunnels.

Between them were other buildings, which in comparison seemed low and squat and were sited to provide ready access to systems of corrals and fenced off pastures in which now some five dozen horses by her quick count were gathered. Set apart was an oval, one-mile track that had on its western side been carved from the hill. Farther to the south she could see the obstacles of a jumping course and farther still more fenced-off land.

It was, she supposed, Greenore Eugenics, and dropping down from the wall, she kept her eyes on the stallion—certainly a thoroughbred in conformation—which, though perhaps a half mile distant, was in the same pasture with her. Perfectly still with its head high and neck arched, it had struck the pose that allowed its normally binocular vision to be transformed briefly into a monocular mode.

But when the animal took first two steps and two more and then began a quick, sustained gallop toward her, Noreen repaired to a fence and climbed over, though she waited for the horse to approach.

It was a clay-colored bay that was stockinged on all four legs up to the cannons.

But what again struck her more than its curious coloring was its regular, athletic-looking shape. Although still a young horse, the animal seemed more thoroughly a thoroughbred to Noreen than any other she had seen in the recent past, including several of the more exceptional animals that were being bred at her father's stud in Dunlavin. She judged that with the exception of its white patches, which were allowable if not desirable, the horse before her seemed to fulfill nearly to perfection the definition of a classic thoroughbred: long, graceful shoulders;

strong quarters; a deep, not thick, rib cage; short cannons with long forearms; and sloping pasterns whose angle was no more than forty-five degrees. Its proportions were exact, and in general it seemed a tight, contained totality.

"Do you have a name?" she asked, as the animal followed her through the now shimmering heat toward the end of its pasture and the stables in the distance. "You do, I know, sure, and you're just being coy," she went on, scanning the other corrals, the buildings, the open bay doors of the stables and seeing nobody about. "Let me guess—Pretty Boy, right? Or"—she picked out a building with some lettering and a shamrock on a sign above the door; she would try there first—"Handsome, Sweet Prince, or Great Form."

At the fence, the stallion pricked its ears and gazed intently toward a pen that contained several fillies. "No, Don Juan," she concluded. "Or, Il Gigolo." She wondered at the horse's history, its pedigree and performance record, if any. Could an animal with such structure and musculature be slow?

The stable area was pristine in its cleanliness but deserted, the interior of the tall Nissen structures vast and comfortably dark in contrast to the harsh glare of the complex from afar. Noreen followed the sound of a radio until, from over tall birthing boxes, she heard a man's voice speaking evidently on a telephone and, she assumed, using the din to mask what he was saying.

"Make s-sense . . . the g-get . . . not the line."

She pressed an ear to the warm side of the stall, directly behind which, she assumed, he was speaking.

"Then where's the a-ad . . ." There was a long, painful pause while the man tried to utter his thought, which burst from him as "-*vantage*. F-fair play to them, let them have him."

A horsefly lit on Noreen's face, and batting at it, she knocked her head against the stall.

"—w-wait—"

She held her breath, looking down the long aisle of horse boxes, the equally long sun-drenched paddock between buildings. There was no place to run.

"—I th-thought I heard . . . No. Listen. I was u-up there. Y-yes, I . . . s-searched everywhere. Nothing, not even the f-false one. T-tom must have t-taken everything. Yes—in the s-safe too.

"All this g-goes nowhere. We must k-keep our . . . eyes on the g-goal, which is the get that we've . . . g-got."

It was difficult even to listen to him, and Noreen tried to consider the frustration that such a disability must cause. Yet it was a big voice and deep.

"Th-theirs is a sh-short term gain, and, sh-sure, let them have it. We've got . . . t-time and all F-Fi's and my f-father's hard work and—" the stutter, which now followed, was desperate and sounded like choking. Finally he blurted out, *History!* Then, "Fionnuala . . ." and ". . . her legacy."

"I'll say no more." This last was said almost with relief, though he seemed to listen and continued, "N-not here, I'm a-a-after t-telling you. B-but . . . can't be far. I'm o-o-off now."

Noreen stole out into the sunlight and hurried toward the next stable and the office building in the distance. She could hear fans whirring, the occasional snort and whinny of horses, and the staticky squawk of the radio, which was squelched after she was safely away. But there had to be other people about, she decided. The place was just too big to have been left unattended, in spite of the death of its owner, and Noreen made straight for the office.

It was, she discovered as she opened the door and

released a freshet of cool air that spilled out on her bare legs, delightfully air-conditioned, and after she stepped in, she paused for a moment to gather herself. How pleasant it would be to sit here for a moment and rest after the long walk up the beach and through the pastures, she thought, but again the quiet drew her forward. Where was all the clatter and flurry of activity of even her father's small operation in Kildare—a typewriter clacking, a phone ringing, certainly voices?

The place was tomblike, and she wondered why. The funeral? Certainly because of the inevitable autopsy and inquest, it could not have been set so soon. A wake? She wondered if the Waltons would choose to observe the custom.

Passing what appeared to be a receptionist's desk, she glanced down at a telephone console. Three circuits were lighted, two of them blinking, which meant that somebody, some place in the building had engaged a line and had two other in-coming calls.

She reached for the receiver but hesitated, and instead moved past the desk into a general office area that contained several desks and off which a carpeted corridor ran to what appeared to be further offices with nameplates on the doors: "J. J. O'Donell, Stable Manager," "Bert Winks, Manager, Sales and Services," "Machala Walton, B.A., Treasurer," "T. A. Daugherty, Manager of Operations," the titles not as yet updated, she assumed, from what Daugherty had told her of his own position with Greenore Eugenics. "Director," he had said.

Then from the end of the hall and office of "Dr. Fionnuala Walton, Ph.D., D.V.M., Director & Breeder," the door of which was open, came the voice of a woman who was, like the man in the stable, obviously on the telephone. As Noreen approached, the woman punched down a phone button and said, "Greenore Eugenics." Her tone was icy and challenging. "No, I'm sorry, Miss Walton is gone for the day. May I have her phone you back?" A pause. "Mr. Daugherty has stepped out as well. I expect him back shortly. May I have your name?" Another pause. "Who *is* this, please?" Then, "Ah, yes—Mr. Yamoudi. Foreign operator four. Certainly, sir. As soon as either returns."

Noreen then heard the click of a phone lever and then another button was punched. "Yes? Yes it is. What? Certainly we'll enter the Newmarket sales, why wouldn't we? What did you say your name was?" The woman piped a high note of pique and slammed the receiver down. "Blast!" she roared, her strong, clear voice resounding up the hall. Noreen heard her snatch up the receiver again. Yet another button was depressed, evidently that of the party she had been speaking to when Noreen had entered the office.

"Janie—the phone is ringing right off the hook, and you know how I can't stand that. Just now somebody saying he was from the press, wanting to know if the rumor is true that Fionnuala Walton has passed away. Odd voice. Dublin accent and very much, you know, citified, like our 'friend' of the hour past."

She listened some more, then, "Certainly I got it. Amn't I the one who compiled the lineage at her request? I put it away myself for safekeeping." Yet another pause, then, "I've just been going through things. You never know what she might have put into the files in one of her . . . *moods,* but where in the name of hell *is* everybody? The place is empty, not a soul as far as I can tell, and we'd be ruined if anybody knew. Destroyed, and not just for breeding horses."

She listened for another while and said, "*Tom?* How dare he suspend operations. He'll have half of Dublin down here, and us with the empty hand. Fionnuala will have put me in charge, and the moment the will is read, he'll get the sack.

"Who? Mna? What could *she* possibly want?" There was yet another pause, then, "Haven't we had enough of her? And, sure, how could she possibly appreciate how much time, money and intelligence went into . . .

"*His* point? Yerra I don't care how much you think of him. You're too easy, too . . . gullible, as I've said time and time again, and do I have to remind you how well-compensated he . . .

"*No!*" It was a cry of outrage. "Do you think they . . . *she?* . . .

"Damn! Here's another call, and I'd best be going. Yes . . . I'll be there."

The woman punched down a button, said, "I'm sorry, Greenore Eugenics has suspended operations for the day. Please call back tomorrow," and crashed the receiver in its yoke.

Noreen, turning in a panic and realizing that she would not have time to flee the building before the woman appeared in the hall, stepped into the dark, open office, near which she was standing, and concealed herself behind the door.

She heard the sounds of something being gathered up and deposited roughly in something else that was metallic. Then the light was switched off, and, peering through the crack of the open door, she saw in the near darkness a figure hurry past. She was about to step out for a better look, when the person appeared again, and, now that her eyes had accustomed themselves somewhat to the dark,

71

Noreen saw a plain black dress, a thin but strong-looking calf wrapped in a nylon stocking, and a single, flat-heeled shoe.

The other office door was closed, and the figure—no more than a blur in the crack of the door—stepped right past Noreen, switched on the overhead light, then switched it off and pulled the door behind which Noreen was hiding closed. Noreen next heard her open, switch the light on, and close every other door down the small corridor.

In the dark Noreen waited, watching square blinking lights appear and pulse and then vanish from the console of the telephone on the desk, wondering why there was no sound. It was, she imagined, more pleasant than the eternal *zing-zing* of the phone in her own place of business, but how much less convenient? One would have to keep glancing in the direction of the phone and when away from it in-coming calls would go unanswered, unless, of course, the bell could be turned on and off and—

Spinning around as with sudden fright, Noreen reached for the knob of the door. Locked. With the tips of her fingers she then made her way, like a blind woman, along the wall until she found a switch, which she threw, and then glanced as quickly as her eyes would allow around the neat, even spartan office of—she remembered —"Machala Walton, B.A."

There was another door that communicated with the office of the dead sister. It was open.

In there too, she quickly found a light switch but discovered that hall door was locked as well. Turning around and glancing toward that desk, she tried to decide what to do. She could telephone Stack or perhaps even her husband at Greenore House, but her value to the inquiry would then be over without her having made a contribution.

What had the woman been searching through? The desk? No, all there was neat. The deep file bin that filled the length of one wall?

Advancing upon it, she found its dozen-plus sections (given the order of the rest of the complex) in disarray: papers protruding from manila envelopes, files dumped back into the bins with labels facing the wall. Half a rack of estrus charts, logging the average five-to-seven-day period in which brood mares would accept stallions and could conceive, were misplaced. Since a mare yielded only one, short-lived egg at the very end of her period of heat, those figures were essential to any economical and efficient breeding of those animals and were treated like holy scripture, at least at her father's stud in Dunlavin.

But where to begin? What to look for? Then, the files of hundreds of mares and hundreds more stallions seemed to be stored there.

And it was only when straightening up in dismay that Noreen took note of something she had been seeing since she first entered the office. It was a wall-sized pedigree chart that had been begun in 1947 with the mating of the famed Broadway Moor, which had been—Noreen now realized—a Walton stallion, with seven mares.

The Moor, as the horse had been called, had been noted for its speed, its stamina over long courses—and, ultimately, for its prepotency. As a stud the horse proved itself capable of passing on its best traits to whole generations of foals, no matter the horse it had been mated with. Noreen's own father had purchased and had had much success with certain of the get of that animal.

As it often happened when a sire's racing and breeding characteristics had proved extraordinary, Broadway Moor had been inbred—Noreen could see on the chart—with his own granddaughters to reinforce his splendid characteristics. But of the other dozens of horses on the chart, only a few did she recognize until she came upon a certain Taghmon.

Beginning only a few years before, according to the chart, that animal had been bred to a series of only the very best mares, from whose families—as Noreen knew for fact because her father himself had nearly paupered his own stud to acquire but one mare of that pedigree—had already come the famed Charlottesville and Sybil's Niece, which in turn meant Admiral's Walk, Nearco, Sister Sarah, Vieux Manoir, Prince Chevalier, and Tulyar were also not so distantly related, or so it was assumed.

What must those mares have cost, Noreen wondered? And why then waste such good blood on this Taghmon, which she was certain now she had never heard of? It was a still-very-much-observed maxim that you bred the best to the best and hoped for the best, but those mares shared nearly the same lineage as Vayrann, Glint of Gold, and Shergar, the great Derby winner, which had been syndicated for ten million pounds sterling. In his second year at stud, the bay stallion had been kidnapped supposedly by the IRA and then destroyed when a ransom had not been paid, or so it was assumed though the horse was never found.

That theft had made the get of horses even distantly related to Shergar all that much more valuable, to say nothing of the foals that Shergar had created in his only season at stud. At auction, one colt out of Galleto by Nijinsky, Noreen most definitely remembered, had brought a sum not previously equaled in Europe of over 300,000 Irish pounds. Her father could speak of nothing else for whole days on end.

But *Taghmon?* And then, as she could see on the chart, to have inbred that horse with its get from those costly mares? Obviously there was something Noreen did not know about this Taghmon.

Glancing up at the chart, she saw that its dam had been one Madame Nora out of Sunbury Prince. Earlier she had noticed an *English General Stud Book* on the desk, and in turning to Madame Nora she then scanned a genealogy that mentioned not one horse that—she believed from her admittedly somewhat limited experience—had distinguished itself any more than, say, having entered important tests with quality horses.

The result? Having garnered the names of the line from the *Stud Book,* she now turned to *Time Form,* the racing periodical, a number of volumes of which were also there in what comprised a kind of handy library. Of the horses related to Taghmon, only two had scored victories in minor races, with two having finished in the money in important victories at Newmarket and Epsom. Both finished third.

Taghmon itself, however, was definitely the best horse of its line. Run as a two-year-old in France, it had finished first in a major test at St. Cloud. Later that month, it won a race among horses of similar promise. The racing sheet ranked the horse 126, a respectable figure but certainly not at the level of the very best horses, which scored in the 130s or higher.

Entered in the Prix de Paris, Taghmon finished in the money, a surprising third, but in the shorter mile-and-a-quarter Prix du Prince d'Orange, the stallion came across a dismal seventh in a field of nine.

Taghmon did not race as a three-year-old, and its service as a stud did not begin until its fourth year, which Noreen again found odd. Few highly valued stallions—

which, given the mares that had since been sent him, he was—"sat out" a year, as it were.

Just then a jingle, which it took Noreen a few seconds to recognize, startled her from her musings, and, as she glanced up, she heard a key mesh into the lock.

In three bounds over the deep plush of the carpet, the blood pounding in her temples so that she felt both giddy and nauseated, she side-stepped lightly behind the door that linked the offices of the two sisters Walton. It was then that the hall door opened.

Forcing her quaking body back into the cold wall, Noreen tried to breathe through her nose and not gasp. And why was she hiding, she asked herself? Hadn't she merely been locked in? A mistake? As she edged close to the crack in the open door, she had to remind herself that she had arrived there because of what her husband, with all his experience, considered a murder.

It was Tom Daugherty, who proceeded directly to and tried the handle of the safe on the wall at the back of the office, then returned to the bins of files. For a moment he considered the disarray there, then stepped to the desk where he picked up the telephone and dialed a number. As it rang, he glanced down at the *Stud Book*, then lowered his head to it. Sweat had seeped through his khaki work shirt, and his tanned forehead was fringed with wet dust. His deep blue eyes then rose to the open door behind which Noreen was concealed and—it seemed to her —met hers for a moment.

"Hello, Bill. Tom Daugherty here. Is my mother about? She said—. Thanks."

Noreen had eased herself back into the wall and now closed her eyes. Shouldn't she walk right out to him and declare her presence? What would she say to him if she remained hidden there through his conversation and then—?

"Ma—all done there? Me too, except the safe is locked." He waited, listening for a few moments. "Yes, I suspect it's she and Siobhan, as we discussed. It couldn't be Deirdre and Dan, though I wouldn't put it past them, chucking a spanner in the works and all. And what in the name of hell —tell me—could *they* do with the beast? Sure, it's better for everybody, can I get him out of the way.

"Listen now—I've that bit of business in Dun Laoghaire now, and I'll be home only to change." He listened, then, "No, no supper, and don't worry—I'll be properly bereaved when the time comes." He listened some more.

"No, not a word of it in Churchtown nor in Broadway. Have you seen the papers?" A pause. "Good. Maybe we'll be lucky, so."

He rang off, and Noreen could feel him—she was sure —hesitate and then stride resolutely toward the open door. He stood there, she saw out of the corner of her eyes —hands on hips, his eyes hooded, his brow furrowed.

He glanced around the office, then turned and snapped out the light there and in the other office too, as he left. He did not close that door.

Sinking down the wall onto her heels, Noreen, who had been born and raised in a family that was profoundly Protestant, waited until she had said a half-dozen Hail Marys and one good Act of Contrition for good measure. Then she left.

6

After making several telephone calls in the village of Kilranell, McGarr again parked his Mini-Cooper at Greenore House, deciding that there were several good reasons why a short walk on a fair day might prove advisable.

First, after a sleepless night and too much smoke and now drink, he needed to clear his head. Also, his Mini-Cooper was not only the ideal small, responsive car for Ireland's narrow roads and laneways, it was an antique of sorts, which was not to be parked with impunity in the yard of a working farm. Finally, it was time to sort things out a bit, at least in regard to the principals and the little he knew to date. Stepping around the forest-green and gray car, McGarr soon found himself out on the sandy, beige road that linked the Walton manse with Binn na Rinn Farms.

There was, of course, the victim herself, Fionnuala Walton, and her two sisters, Siobhan and Machala, and the niece, Deirdre. It only now struck him how definite the contrast between their Irish given names and their English surname. But then their father had been a patriot and had fought in the Revolution, so they said. From their say-so as well, only they and Mna Daugherty and her two sons, Tom and Dan Jr.—the history of which family was so inextricably bound to the Waltons—had had access to the victim on or about the time of her death.

Which was? Just about now, McGarr had been told over the phone by the pathologist—"Half-two or three in the afternoon"—a day past. McGarr kicked a stone into the weeds and knocked up the brim of his hat. It was hot on the road in the lee of tall hedgerows. The toes of his woven-leather brogues were now tan with dust.

The victim: she had been a university-trained eugenicist and doctor of veterinary medicine. She had also been founder, owner, and director of a horse-breeding facility with an international reputation. Then, she had herself owned at least five hundred choice acres that were valuable both as cropland and because of their contiguity to the sunniest sandy beaches in the entire island. She had been, therefore, a wealthy and successful woman, and he wondered if her murder had been in some way connected to her holdings.

Doffing his jacket, which he tucked with the vinyl case under one arm, McGarr turned and looked back at her house that was imposed in angular silhouette upon a cerulean blue sky. Could he possibly be out of breath after such a short walk, he wondered?

Then she, the victim, had been by the sisters' report a passionate, tenacious woman who had attempted to "control" (Machala's word) every aspect of life that touched hers, most particularly that of her erstwhile fiancé turned employee/partner. By means of a complex net of business, professional, and (McGarr did not doubt, given Siobhan's statements about the dead woman's unconventionality) personal obligations, she bound him perhaps even tighter than by mere marriage. She then employed

79

his sons and her one sister in her business and the other in the capacity of menial in her house, or so it now seemed to McGarr. "Too early," he murmured to the dust at his feet.

Then there was the niece, Deirdre, who in her betrothal seemed to be replaying right down to the name of the man she would marry the victim's experience. McGarr wondered how much Fionnuala Walton had had to do with that arrangement and how she had felt about it. It had been said (again by Machala) that the impending marriage but a week distant was another subject that Mna Daugherty and the victim might have discussed at their meeting on the afternoon of the death the day before. Why so soon before the marriage? Had they not spoken of it before? Arrangements? Expenses? From what he had been told and could gather of their lives, he did not think that either woman would have left many of the financial details to chance. Plainly, he did not know enough.

He did know, however, certain hard facts. The victim had been struck at least twice with the heavy, forged head of a farrier's claw, the first blow (he assumed) striking the victim's forearm, the second her left cheek. The force of the blows either drove her out onto and off the landing or she—could it have been?—had afterward been flung down the steep flight of stairs.

The head of that same farrier's claw, which carried traces of blood and bits of the skin of the victim, had been used to pry up the tacks in the edge of the carpet at the top of the stairs. It had ruptured the varnish there, forcing flakes into the crevice of its claw. It had then been replaced beside the other horseshoeing implements on the peg behind the door.

Because of the dust in the attic, the killer had seen fit to wipe clean much of the floor and an area high on the wall. One footprint of a woman's square-toed shoe, size five, remained. Though the shaft of the farrier's claw at some point in the recent past had also been wiped clean, two clear fingerprints remained over the dusty track of the rag that had been used for the cleaning—the thumb and index finger of a right hand. Prints like it had been found in the bedroom of the niece, Deirdre, though when McGarr had observed her and young Daugherty in the attic, neither had touched the implement. Then, why not the fourth digit with a hand which—McGarr supposed—was small? What sort of grasp was necessary to wield the tool as a weapon?

But then why had the niece, who was supposedly napping in her room not more than fifty feet from the final resting place of the victim, not heard the fall? Even with the rug, the report must have been more than simply loud. Had she gone out to young Daugherty, wherever he had been waiting to take his turn at the victim's ear? And then, what was it the niece had said to him, there in the attic?

"I thought you—" her eyes had searched his face, as though in confirmation of her fears. Then, "And you know why—don't tell me you don't." And finally, ". . . when in all of your family and mine she was probably the only true friend we had."

Siobhan, then, and Machala and Tom Daugherty were not to be considered friends? Nor his own mother, Mna? Why not? Because of the "control" the victim had exercised over their lives? And over Deirdre's and young Daugherty's lives, what sort of hold was that beyond the fact of having housed the one and employed the other? Then, whose daughter was Deirdre anyhow? Had he gotten that sister's name, McGarr now asked himself, wondering just how much farther Binn na Rinn Farms could possibly be? No—he realized, now removing his handkerchief from his pocket to mop his brow—but he would.

And Siobhan herself: where had she been that she had not heard her sister's fall—down in the kitchen with Tom Daugherty at least for a time, so she'd said. Far enough away from the third-story landing not to have heard? Perhaps, though after a life of some sixty-plus years in the house would she not have been acquainted with every noise inside or out? Had she not been interested in the exact purpose of Mna Daugherty's visit, the length of her stay, and whatever resolution or lack of one that might have resulted?

When had Machala left, before Tom or after him, as she claimed? Tiring of waiting for his mother's meeting with the victim to end, he had—by Siobhan's say-so—gone out the back, walking across the fields to the horse-breeding facility to the south. From the window over her sink she had watched him depart.

And Machala? Supposedly she was already there, back at work.

Placing the handkerchief back in his jacket pocket, his hand touched the notes which he had taken during his telephone call to Technical Squad headquarters in Dublin. Opening the sheet, he glanced down at the findings: the memorabilia in the trunks, which had been rifled through, had been touched either with the back of a finger or some object, like a stick (or a farrier's claw, thought McGarr). It was as though whoever had conducted what, he assumed, had been a quick, anxious search had known what he was after. There had been pages removed from certain of the journals and a page from the family Bible.

On the floor were traces of the same sort of oil that was found on the shaft of the claw, though the identity of the substance was not yet known. Also discovered were bits of gravel, sand, horse droppings, one complete pellet and the chip from a second of the fertilizer 5-10-5, some bits of straw, and three slivers and a .5-mm. piece of prismatic glass, which was also being further tested.

The gravel, sand, horse droppings, etc., could easily have come in on his own shoes or Stack's or the niece's or her fiancé's. In any case, it wasn't much, McGarr concluded, as he drew up under an immense chestnut tree. Like a cooling shower, its deep shade fell on him, and he doffed his cap and again mopped his brow. Leaning into the bank from which the tree had first grown but now largely formed, he was loath to admit that he felt a bit dizzy after—how few could it have been?—one or at most two miles. Yet, he felt *better* than he had, say, upon getting out of the car at Greenore House, and not poorly enough to refuse a drink, were one offered.

In fact, he thought, a wee taste might do him very nicely, though he refrained from tapping the flask which he had refreshed at a pub in Kilranell. After his seventeen-day abstinence, he would rekindle his habit slowly but not—mind—as an obeisance to any or all of his several critics. Damn them. And why had he ever first let anybody question what had been for him merely a fact of life, the way he was, a pleasant pastime that allowed him to muse?

Then, you know, it was good weather for thinking, he thought as, stretching, he raised his eyes into the deep green bowers, heavy with lighter colored burrs that in fall would split open to drop the chestnuts that he savored roasted with sherry in an iron pan. The tree was, in fact, the first of an avenue that ran the gentle curve of the road toward the Daugherty abode and must have been planted at least a century before the Edwardian

Greenore House had been built. Two, perhaps.

Also the structure of the older farmhouse, which could just be seen through the deep shade of the tree canopy, was curious for Ireland. It reminded McGarr that Wexford had been the first county permanently subdued by the Normans and, given its gently rolling hills, its roads that followed the borders of fields, and its many small, neat, slate-roofed houses, the area appeared more characteristically English than most other parts of the country.

Likewise, the farmhouse before him was a rambling, additive structure in which barns that had been appended to the house had been made into rooms and further barns constructed of fieldstone and rock until the house sprawled in both directions. The roof of the central section was slated, while both wings were still in thatch. Even the pebbling of the facade was various, but painted white to present a unified front, and under a high, blue sky and framed by the magnificent chestnuts, it was the sort of place that, glimpsed from afar like this, made McGarr's imagination posit whole centuries of fruitful history for the family within.

How much, if at all, did that ideal square with the reality, he wondered, though he now did not doubt that the farmstead predated Greenore House as the Waltons' (the controlling family's) dwelling until (he was guessing) somewhat after the turn of the present century. In such a way the architectural extravagance of Greenore House might be considered a "folly," since the land and the setting nearly demanded an intensively applied agronomy and little else. When had the Daughertys established themselves there and under what conditions? Had they themselves been the "original" inhabitants of this countryside, McGarr wondered, though in Ireland it was now rare to discover a family that had survived the country's centuries of conquest and subjection, its disasters and evictions, in one place.

The brass knocker, doorknob, and kickplate of the frosted-glass front door had been polished to a luster, its panels recently painted a high-gloss ivory. The details of the rest of the facade, though, had been largely ignored. There were paint chips on the sills. A rose bush had climbed a trellis to the eaves.

McGarr rapped on the glass and turned to the driveway. A kind of shrine, looking like a birdbath, stood forlorn in an expanse of limestone gravel that had strayed in among plantings and under the chestnuts. Noreen's Deux Chevaux looked like a toy beside a new, mud-spattered Mercedes Turbo. Black with tinted windows, the larger car looked like a hearse.

A short, stocky woman wearing an apron over a plain, black dress answered the door. "Yes?" she asked, the space between her two front teeth wide. It seemed to repeat the line that parted glossy finger waves of black hair. Her nose was a pert knob; her jaw was square. With a smile of pleasant though not uncritical curiosity, her jet eyes took in McGarr's dusty brogues, damp shirt and—as he removed his cap—his sweat-beaded and balding brow.

"Mrs. Daugherty?"

She nodded.

"I've come on two matters. The first is more immediately pressing. I require accommodations."

An eyebrow arched, her forehead wrinkled. Birdlike, her head moved to one side and she scrutinized him intensely. "Do you now?" She glanced out into the driveway. "For how many?"

"Myself alone."

"For how long?"

"I have no idea yet. At least several days. Say, three for now."

"You come on foot?"

McGarr felt like a bug under glass. From down a dark hall wafted the rich, sweet odor of braised beef, boiled cabbage, and potatoes. There some other women were conversing above the clatter of pots and plates.

Faintly, as in obbligato, he could just make out the sweet, toasty odor of dark barmbrack. "It's such a fair day, I left my car back on the road."

She paused a moment as though making a judgment, then asked, "At Greenore House, by any chance?"

"How did you guess?"

"And the second matter?"

"Fionnuala Walton."

She stepped back. "Right this way."

In a small sitting room, the spartan black walnut and leather appointments of which reminded McGarr of a doctor's surgery, she paused by the door. "Tea?" she asked. "Coffee? Or could I offer you somethin' stronger?"

"Only if you are," McGarr replied with an alacrity that rather disturbed him. Was it because he knew that a woman of her background would not refuse him or because his first aim was to keep the interview informal? "And my name is Peter McGarr." As with the session at Greenore House, he wanted all she could tell him.

"Of the Gárda?" she asked, pouring two healthy drinks and handing a glass to him.

McGarr nodded.

"And your rank?"

"I'm from Dublin Castle."

Her head seemed to sink, and for one who seemed so robust, she sat demurely on the edge of one of the chairs. Drawing her feet, which were small, together, she crossed

her ankles. "Then it's murder, and you've come to me."
She glanced up, and McGarr fixed her gaze with eyes
which could be, he knew, as cold and unblinking as any.

"You were the last to see her alive." From the case he
withdrew the same three items that he had shown the
Walton sisters: the bottomless bottle, the wedding portrait
of Fionnuala and the man who had instead become the
husband of the woman before him, and, finally, the farrier's claw that he believed had been used in the murder.

Easing his back into the firm slats of the chair, McGarr
tasted the malt and waited.

Raising her glass to him, Mna Daugherty drank off the
whiskey without a tremor or twinge or her eyes in any
way straying from his, and McGarr wondered if the toast
were a kind of challenge. As she stood to get herself another, she began speaking.

"That first thing is a blower, what people around here
use to keep things fair and equal when it comes to marriage. It was, as you probably know since it's been a full
day now and you've brought it to me, my own salvation
—what kept me from London or Brighton or wherever I
might have gone, a young, unmarried woman with her
bastard spawn, and whatever I might have had to do to
keep . . . Tom and me whole.

"And I would have too—know that. Anything. For it's
flesh that counts and what's real and negotiable in this
world, and there was nothing me father or brothers
couldn't or wouldn't have done to keep me from being
wronged."

The crystal decanter—horribly ornate, one of the more
unfortunate Waterford designs—rang on the lip of the
matching glass, and reaching for the one that McGarr
held, she as much as tugged it from his grasp. She topped
it up.

"And wronged I was, I'm here to say," she continued, resuming her seat and again meeting McGarr's stare. The black straps of the summery shoes that matched her dress bound the flesh of her feet, like thongs the heads of stone war clubs. The shoes had rounded toes, not square, but McGarr guessed they were size five. "Just sixteen, mind, and impressionable by a man who was then nearer my father's age and who'd been hired on by him to tutor me for my exams. He had aspirations that I become something other than a poor, Wexford farmer's wife, he did. For, you see"—she swirled the liquor in the glass and smiled slightly—"I had the brains for the training and all I wanted was the"—she looked away—"application." She smiled, rather fancying her choice of word.

"From the first, though, he flirted or at least—I suppose, and I want you to understand this as it was—I interpreted it that way. It was his nature, I believe: to please. And"—she let out a small sharp laugh, rocking back in the seat, the fresh glass raised to her lips, her smile that crabbed a system of lines at the corners of her eyes focused at some point above McGarr's head in a manner that, he judged, was not solely histrionic. —"please me he did one day in my father's sitting room when on a day like today with everybody else out haying, I began pulling at his curls and, like the soldier he had been, he turned me down on my back, pulled up my skirts, and fooked me proper there and then and every time we met—at the crossroads, in the barn, his motor car, the beach, even when I'd get riding and meet him on the tractor out in the fields. One night he took me out to Carnsore Point and laid me down on the rock on the very top.

"And listen to me while I tell ya," she went on, lifting herself up to slide a leg under a thigh and turning her eyes, which were sparkling, back on McGarr, "it was only right that he should marry me and not Fionnuala and not just because he got me with child that very first time there on the carpet. I'll swear to it.

"No. It was that, although Dan and her were a well-suited pair in regard to their interests, which was horses and the land that had been, bye and bye, all Daugherty property, Dan and *me* were a *natural* pair, and I'll tell you what I mean. Like"—again the smile—"hand in glove, if you'll pardon me drift. There was hardly a night that went by—come day, go day, year in and year out right up almost until his death—that we didn't act like man and wife, if ye're with me, Peter?"

She laughed again. "Really. Religion, background, blood—we were the *real* Irish who had been here in these parts, our two families, from year one. Then there wasn't a thought that he had or a feeling I didn't know. When he was hungry or thirsty or tired or needed me or the boys or a drink"—she eyed McGarr's glass, which he had not again sipped from—"I understood and without, mind, his having to give me a nudge. And all that passed between us without words. Nary a one.

"Fionnuala?" She gestured toward the wedding picture. "Sure, I can, I could understand her . . . *love* for him, and his . . . regard for her. What more important could she have been to us than our bread and buther, and by her—rather—*through* her we achieved, God save us"—her hand swept out—"the little we have. If for that Dan let her believe she meant something special, if they had"—her eyes swung to him and searched his face, a slight wrinkle appearing on her brow—"projects together, if in fact (and who am I to gainsay it) he raised her skirts reg'-lar, she deserved every little touch, but I'll tell you this.

"Dan was a good man in his own way and true. He never stinted me or his own. And, sure, what's a bull for but service. It would have been a shame to have let the blood of that man, who as a husband and a provider and as—you know—just plain good company was the best, languish." Her eyes were suddenly glassy, and she tossed back her drink.

"The third thing there," she said in a voice suddenly gone high, "is a farrier's claw, which I haven't seen the like of since Dan stopped using his in the Fifties, I think.

"Now—drink up, sir. All this chat has parched me pipe, and I'll have another, I will, though I shouldn't." Wondering if she was trying or really thought she could get him drunk, McGarr complied, and, saying, "That's a lad," she stepped to the decanter.

When she had resumed her seat, he asked, "But yesterday, Mna—may I call you that—?"

"Sure, you can call me anything but an ungrateful bitch, which at least *I*'m not."

"—why did you arrange to see her?"

"Is that what's on every tongue at Greenore House, when it wasn't all me, you know. It was mutual, it was.

"Ya see, we'd been having a wrangle, and I'll make no bones about that either." Tiny red patches had appeared on her cheeks. "They've probably run through it from their side already, but it was about the land she claimed was leased and I had optioned and all but bought. It had been, you see, an arrangement—word of mouth—between her and Dan himself, and 'twas known to half the county. A lease/*purchase* agreement over a twenty-year term, poor Dan dying a year and a half before he could take title."

"On how many acres?"

"Muscha, the whole lot that we'd been planting under straight rent—keep that foremost—since the early Fifties and lease/purchase these eighteen and a half years. Sure, they were—they *are*—ours by use, and weren't they just taken from us to begin with."

"Five hundred or so acres?"

She nodded, her eyes narrowing down on his lips as if to read his expression. "That would have been lying fallow and not good to man nor beast without us, save for the odd"—she waved a hand—"t'oroughbred saddle horse fit for nothin' but some t'in jockey's bony arse. And her with her 'incremental values' and 'amortization tables' and the like, when we were speaking of some of the best land in all the country and the bounty that could be provided for all—her and hers included—from it. Yes"—she nodded her head vehemently—"*gain*, which is not yet a dirty word from what I hear, though from hard work and hard work alone."

Again she was up and advancing on the decanter with a rolling, almost truculent gait.

Said McGarr, "And there yesterday—was it in the attic? —you asked her what?"

"*Asked* nothing, man. Mna Daugherty goes hat in hand to neither woman nor man. I"—she paused for a moment, searching for a word—"*proposed* a straight swap." The crystal again resounded. "She to kick in the sale of the land, as a kind of dowry like to the marriage. A . . . shall we say, *peace* offering between two families that were about to be joined in marriage, like she herself almost was?"

Puzzled by her use of the conditional tense, McGarr turned so he could see her directly. She had opened her hands, as though raising her palms to the wall behind the table that held the decanter. Her eyes were partially closed. It was as if even now she could appreciate the perfection of her proposal. "Would she just release the acreage, for the fair price that we'd been payin' on, mind, over twenty-plus years *with* an additional five hundred quid per acre, just to show my heart was in the right place?

"For that, sure, the whole, blessed family would agree to this marriage and in the best faith see those two children joined. In that way the . . . 'partnership,' like it was in Dan's day and now in Tom's and"—there was a slight pause—"Dan Junior's," she nodded, repeating, "Dan Junior's, too, would continue."

She then looked down at her glass, which McGarr waited for her to top up before he said, "I'm only a poor policeman and a city fella, unused to the subtleties of country life. Why *should* the Waltons supply a dowry, as you phrase it, when, as it is, they're bringing a great house, a choice tract of property, an internationally reputable business and—so I've heard—an heiress to this marriage?"

As though trying to clear her head, Mna Daugherty inspired several deep breaths that swelled the angular rake of her considerable chest. How old was she, he wondered? His own age or a bit older, though what he suspected was that steady, arduous labor had kept her fit.

Returning to her chair, she sat. "But we don't know that, do we? Fionnuala was cute, she was, with her givings and takings, her 'you'll have this on these conditions, which I might withdraw at any time.' It was the way she kept things close, so—Dan and then Tom and finally Dan Junior with that little slattern of a niece.

"And not being a woman who leaves anything to chance when it comes to Binn na Rinn Farms, I decided I should make things definite before"—there was yet another pause, then she added with slightly drunken hurry —"the marriage. Dan, you see, is a good boy and me own and a Daugherty, but—" Seemingly aware that McGarr's eyes were on her, she waited, then made a fist so that her bicep, which a short sleeve exposed, swelled. "—mine is the surer hand.

"And wouldn't you know," she continued, her features suddenly brightening, *"she went for it."* When McGarr cocked his head, she explained, "The letter of intent. I took it to my solicitor, who will file it with the court."

McGarr doubted the value of any document signed on the day—hell, perhaps even the hour—of a person's murder, should the deceased's heir choose to contest it. Then, of course, some other finding might more totally disallow the petition, he reminded himself.

"Your son, Dan. He had arranged to see the victim as well."

She looked away. "Yes. After me."

"Why?"

Her mood as suddenly somber, she turned to McGarr. "I suppose that was a matter between her and him. Or, now, you and him."

What was he hearing, an accusation? Astonished that her familial regard, which had seemed total, had now more than simply vanished, he finished his drink and stood. "A young lad, is he?" he asked as they approached the door.

"The word. The very word. And him a *scholar* like, though his affliction—have you met him, Peter?"

McGarr shook his head.

"—the affliction, you'll see, only makes it worse. Sure, he'd have the world entire in his pocket, could he learn it to jump."

McGarr wondered if the boy considered Deirdre Walton, Greenore House, and Greenore Eugenics the world entire. Certainly it was a large part of his mother's.

He reached for the doorknob, but she placed a hand on it, turning her head to him as though to speak in earnest.

"We don't really get on, you'll soon learn. Dan Junior and me. Not since his father died. It's something, I'm told, fatherless boys go through. His brother, Tom, has tried to take him in hand, but he's young and handsome and looks more like his father than—"

"How did you leave the victim?"

She blinked, then smiled, "On my feet, of course. Whew! The drink." She touched the tips of her fingers to her upper chest. Because all too feminine, it was another gesture which seemed affected. "Sure, the less bitten, the sharper the pain. It's got me reeling, it has—where were we? Ah, yes—the *victim*, as you say. A veritable brick, to tell you true, upon me last sight of her."

"Which was where?"

Her eyes, which were as clear as the moment McGarr had walked in, shied. "The attic, where she made me bully these old bones so we could commiserate over Dan's 'mementoes,' said she, like two old shrews over a grave. And worse, I'll tell ya, but not for the public ear: I think she might have gone a bit off, there at the end," she whispered. "She showed me this chart, just like down at the Eugenics, but instead of having horses on it, it had people. She kept going on about Dan and how prepotent she thought he'd prove. She even began speaking of Dan and Deirdre's 'get,' such that I had to smile. I tell you, after a while I'd had enough, but, you know, it was in the spirit of . . . conciliation, as I told you. And wasn't she a kind-hearted woman and just, now, in the end, God bless her. Doin' the decent thing by us and the farm and all."

"What time did you leave?"

"Sir—you think me the sort of woman who's always consulting a clock?" She had a hand on McGarr's sleeve, and she had turned her head to look into his face. "I'm still just a jolly girl at heart, happy-go-lucky, who expects nothing more than a little fun out of life."

McGarr's eyes searched her face. What was he hearing, a proposition? They were, of course, more or less the same age and he suspected the woman could not have had many "opportunities," as it were, in the recent past.

"But let me assure you this—like all people who do things and not just talk of them, I've been called many names in me time but a murderess never onc't and never will. And upon my word Fionnuala Walton was when I saw her first and last yesterday afternoon in one very agreeable piece. If I got there at half one, I couldn't have stayed more than an hour."

McGarr heard the front door open, and somebody stepped into the hall.

"Now then." Opening the sitting room door, Mna Daugherty brushed against McGarr. "Shall I show you to your room, Inspector?"

"Why not," said McGarr, stepping out and nearly into his wife, who with flushed cheeks was hurrying down the hall.

"Hi"—she blurted out and then with a blink forced her green eyes beyond him—"Mrs. Daugherty."

"Mna, dear. Just call me Mna. Where're ya rushin' to?"

"Well"—she blushed—"your son, Tom, has invited me to dinner and then a bash on a yacht, and"—her eyes strayed to McGarr—"I'm late." Whether it was the whiskey or happening upon her unexpectedly, like this, McGarr did not know. But with her tan and the color in her cheeks and her eyes lively, she looked no different and perhaps even more youthful than on the day McGarr first met her nine years before.

And he was suddenly filled with a great, inexplicable longing for her and the dream that they had had of what they could mean to each other and which presented itself, like a pleasant prospect seen from a distance: of how their life could be together, day by day, minute by minute. Given the multiplicity of their lives and the fact that they had to work for their living, it was, of course, an impossible dream, but somehow, he there and then promised himself, they would have to get back at least to the pursuit of the ideal. Which was? He could now remember only a vague feeling of what it had been.

"Dinner?" the woman inquired. "My dinner isn't for" —plunging a hand into her bodice, she produced a fat, gold pocket watch held by a string—"forty-five minutes. I mean, supper."

Flustered, Noreen explained. "In Wexford, I'm afraid. Some gorgeous place, so he says, though we'll see, we will."

Mna Daugherty did not introduce them, and Noreen turned down the hall.

"Great to be young, isn't it, inspector? Let me guide you to your digs," which with the rays of westering sun through fluffy curtains was a fuzz of brilliant, chartreuse light.

"Supper's at half six." She checked the attached toilet and smoothed the three lime-green towels, which banded the back of an ultramarine chair. "I'm down to the pub in the village tonight. Care to come along?"

McGarr said he had other plans, and it was not long before he heard the happy-go-lucky-girl-at-heart barking orders in the kitchen with a vehemence that a sergeant-major might envy.

She was—he did not doubt, settling himself into the chair without removing the towels—an intense, two-fisted, busy person who drank readily and often. It only exaggerated her salient characteristics, which were immoderate greed and the same need to control that Fionnuala Walton had been accused of. When the latter was alive, Greenore Point must have been some lively place, he imagined. And then poor Dan Daugherty Sr., caught between two such *unusual* women. It was little wonder they survived him.

Toeing off his dusty brogues, he tried to conceive of what, beyond the sure sexual exchange, Daugherty and his *Woman*—the literal meaning of *Mna* in Irish—might have had in common. For many Irishmen, a strict non-verbal fulfillment of essential, nonverbal needs was an ideal in marriage. Who needed a woman's talk, her complaints, the gossip, and meddling? A clean house, a hot meal, and the care of one's children was the most one could expect, and if, as she described it, a "*good* fook" was tossed in nightly (as she had it), so much the better.

And there—he thought, pulling the short brim of his cap down in an attempt to screen out the green light—his young wife who was in no way *that* ideal, was going to dinner and who knew where else with such a woman's son.

McGarr had scarcely removed the cap of the flask when his eyes began to close. Yet he managed a final, numbing sip.

Well, he thought as he settled into a delicious sleep—I may not be much meself, but at least I'm me. Once again.

7

W exford. *Weis-fjord.*

In the gloaming, the wide bowl of its harbor, named by the Vikings, was filled with light. Directly above Noreen and Tom Daugherty was the sharp, achromatic disc of a newly risen, full moon in a starry sky. To the north was the pale, azure glow which, because of Ireland's latitude, would remain for most of the night. Finally there was the yacht, which was anchored so far off the shore that the sounds of the orchestra and party aboard were weak and intermittent, coming to Noreen and Tom Daugherty on a gentle breeze as they waited with other guests to be lightered across the calm water. Through some system of submarine illumination, its hull glowed phosphorescent and pure in a jadelike flux that shimmered and made the vessel seem ethereal. A vision.

Behind them on the jetty where the Mercedes was parked among other expensive cars, a crowd that otherwise would have been fishing or strolling had gathered to watch the party guests depart. They made Noreen feel rather special.

First, Daugherty had had the car cleaned and polished and had even plumped for a driver in uniform. Then, his tuxedo was new and appeared to have been tailored to his angular body, his graying hair was freshly clipped, and his fingernails were manicured. And the way the precise collar with its bold black tie set off his dark features was almost startling. The others on the jetty, even those waiting for the lighter, could scarcely keep their eyes from him, and in no way—Noreen concluded—did he seem a product of Binn na Rinn Farms.

"Who's that?" one of the onlookers on the jetty had asked, when the driver had opened a back door of the Mercedes. "Amn't I after seeing him on . . ." the woman had then named a popular British melodrama. "No—it's the bloke who owns the bloody boat, I'm tellin' yuh. Greek, like the name of the thing. I saw him meself out on the fantail of it, up in Dun Laoghaire this afternoon. All khakis, he was. A gold chain round his neck and on his wrist—*there,* you can see it now." Daugherty had reached for Noreen's hand to help her from the car.

"And wouldn't you know it," said somebody else in the crowd that had gathered around the limousines and sports cars, "him with a genuine, Irish mistress." It was as though they were watching an event on television, or they believed Noreen and Daugherty did not possess ears. "Look at her eyes and that hair and that dress." It was silk and sheer and the same deep green color of her eyes. "Sure—she's the woman for a wild, summer night, I'd say. Brilliant and expensive. Where'd she get that necklace?"

"Where d'you think? A trophy, you can bet, but—God —they look good enough to eat. The both a dem."

And far different from the impression almost of father and daughter that was created when she was with her husband, she thought, as Daugherty, with an ease that also surprised her, guided them through the crowd to the edge of the jetty. Again she wondered what it would have been like to have married a handsome, "sporting" man more her contemporary and lived a healthy, open life in the country among some people who shared their tastes and activities.

They would hunt in the fall, fish in the spring. In the winter they would pop over to Norway for a long, arduous trek on cross-country skis, then down to Ibiza for sun and rest. They would have a houseful of kids, an estate filled with animals.

It was not the first time she had considered the ideal, and now it seemed all too attractive. "Flattered?" he asked.

"Me?" She shook her head. "It's the car. Does it every time. And there all along I thought it was Mammy's."

"*My* mammy's?" he asked, his eyes playful, his smile warm. "My mammy *drives*—my car, your car if you let her and I can recommend you refuse when she asks, which if you're with us long enough, please God, she will —but never *her* car, which does not and never will exist. When I was young she drove tractors and combines, and I once saw her drive a cattle lorry to market when our 'help' was being obstreperous enough to demand extra money for extra work. Far be it from me to run Mammy down, but she retains to this day the unfailing ability to hire docile men who possess automobiles and cannot say no, at least to her."

"And your father?"

"Well—here I am, living proof that her power worked on him, when he was foolish enough to come within range, which wasn't often."

"But the room, the one I'm staying in, is expensively done and—"

"Garish," Daugherty supplied.

"Well—I was thinking of the phrase, 'carefully considered.' And then, of course, there's her pocket watch. The gold alone in that must be worth a few quid."

"That's Dan's, my father's, and should have been mine, which puts her in the proper perspective, I should think." Daugherty's smile had fallen somewhat. "It was the first thing she removed from his person. That is, she removed his watch and wallet and then determined that his body was in fact a corpse. It's another of her talents. Invariably she knows when a cow, a horse, a business enterprise or even sometimes"—he looked off toward the lighter, which was approaching—"even a person is dying. She has 'The Eye,' as some would have it in these parts, though there's nobody brave enough to say it to her face."

There was a pause as the lighter, itself a sizable boat, gave three blasts that resounded off the stone of the breakwater and echoed across the harbor.

"Those rooms?" He obviously meant the guest rooms at his mother's house. "All first quality and purchased by blind telephone orders. 'Hello, Brown Thomas?' " he mimicked, naming Dublin's dearest department store. " 'Send me four dozen of your best terry-cloth bath towels. Colors? Of course, you eedjit, and the brighter the better. And chandeliers, now. I'm the woman for the odd chandelier, I am, and I'll have mine large. The goriest you have. And milkmaids and shepherds and, I was t'inking—have you anything half-man and half-beast, like in the *aaahrt* books. I'll take a dozen. No, make it three.'

"But to answer your question"—as though taken by the play spirit of their conversation, Daugherty reached down and picked up her left hand, which he turned over, examining the back of it—"when Mammy *does* buy a car —an event, the dramatic possibilities of which she will not in one lifetime be able to ignore—it will be no mean sardine tin, like mine. A Rolls, at the very least. Or a Bugatti, and if that isn't long enough, a hearse with silver wings and lots of chrome.

" 'Hello, Dee-troit, this is Mna Daugherty over here at Binn na Rinn Farms in County Wexford. Where, you ask? Why *Ireland,* you oaf, and come closer now while I tell ya and listen sharp. You know them gold Eldorados the rock stars have, the ones with the bar, the telly, and the platinum wheels. I'll take one. No, two. In a pinch I'll use the other as a guest room.' "

"But why?" Noreen asked, when she had finished laughing.

"The parsimony on the one hand, the . . . awkward ostentation on the other?" He cocked his head in a thoughtful way that made him seem to her even more appealing than when he smiled. "I've thought about it but not often, mind, and I always conclude that she doesn't know herself or that she's a person who has no self-conscious thoughts. She functions by means of urges, which come through for her when it matters but when it doesn't —? Well, you have those rooms."

Noreen's brow furrowed, as the gangway dropped onto the jetty wall. "When, pray, does it matter?"

Daugherty shook his head, and as the others made way for them, he took Noreen's arm and directed her into the boat. "That's hard to say, for it varies from year to year. But any big, essential purchase—a new tractor or combine or a prize bull." He almost began to laugh. "Or, years back, my apprenticeship to my former career or Dan's 'training' and later his education or anything, like that, she never stinted—*whenever* our 'Aunt' Fi did not come forward." His eyes flashed at Noreen, who kept looking at the yacht in the distance.

"Your *former* career?" she asked, raising their hands

and turning them over as he had before, so she could examine the back of his hand. She decided that she had better dispense with the fact, obvious in the band of white skin on the third finger of her right hand, that she was married. If, as Daugherty had said, his connection to the Greek shipping magnate, whose vessel they were now approaching, was horses, then doubtless she would know at least a few of the people aboard. Ireland was a small place and the horsing world smaller still.

"A jock, I'm afraid," said Daugherty. "From around age fourteen to twenty-four or -five when I finally matured and became a pillar of steel and about as heavy." He made a fist of their hands.

"Good training for a breeder," Noreen suggested.

"Not nearly so as marriage."

"Does it disturb you?"

"No"—he cocked his head again and smiled in a way that left no doubt of its suggestion—"not in the least. As in a horse, I prefer a little experience in a woman. It makes them more . . . appreciative and *tractable.*"

Because of the implication of the remark, their eyes met with a force that left Noreen somewhat breathless. They were standing close together and his thigh against hers made her tingle. "Appreciative of what, sir?" She could not keep her eyes from flickering down on his lips.

"Any little thing I can do for her. Flowers. A dance." They could now hear every note of the orchestra on the afterdeck of the vessel. "A romp round the meadow."

"At Binn na Rinn Farms?" Almost as though she had already decided on the indiscretion, Noreen's mind considered the complication of her husband's presence in some other, nearby room and how any "discovery" might be averted. She blushed with shame. She could now feel a certain dampness on her forehead. She felt dizzy and at once wanted to keep holding and wanted to throw off his hand.

"Why there?" he asked.

"Well—you're master there, are you not, and—"

"Me *master* of Binn na Rinn Farms?" he laughed. "I'll tell that one to my mother, I will."

She explained, grateful for the chance to change the subject, "I mean, you will be someday when—"

Daugherty shook his head and slipped his hand around her waist, ostensibly to steady her as the lighter rolled into the tall hull of the yacht. The hand moved lower still, and she reached for it. "Not me. Dan maybe, though it would seem he'll be well enough placed as it is, if—" His features glowered, and she felt his grip on her relax.

"But it's a huge place, is it not? How many acres—hundreds and hundreds, and then your family's been there for—"

"Far too long," he laughed. "It's gotten so we're moldering here, and then I've got other, better plans and"—he winked at her—"bigger. Ones that are larger in horizon." He glanced up at the lights of the yacht. "And, sure—you'd not want to be known as the mistress of a farmer, would you now?"

Nor of a murderer, she thought.

"Your husband—tell me about him. What does he do in —is it Dublin?"

Asking herself what might be "larger in horizon" than a good, big farm on some of the best and most picturesque land in the entire country, Noreen stepped toward the yacht's gangway, which was a kind of pneumatic lift that carried them to the deck of the vessel. After all, in his present situation Daugherty was working for somebody else.

"I never speak of my husband. Never," she said and

wondered why even mentioning him to Daugherty made her feel both guilty and sad.

His two careers, however, explained why, once aboard the *Amphitrite*, Tom Daugherty was so familiar and comfortable with most of the guests that it seemed as though he was their host instead of the small man with the sallow face and world-weary eyes.

In fact, of all aboard the vessel, Nick B. Athos, who Daugherty said now based his operations in Australia, seemed least likely to be its owner. While the others spoke and joked with each other, danced and talked, Athos prowled the salon and deck, taking a seat which, it appeared, he found uncomfortable, and then another and another. Even his smile—a kind of baring of teeth—seemed uneasy.

Then, he neither drank the champagne that was flowing freely nor smoked the Havana cigars that his stewards, clad in sea-green jackets with white ties to match the colors of the superstructure, kept offering. He only nodded his head and extended a limp hand, when introduced, then tugged at a lapel of his evening jacket, as though it felt as ill-fitting as it looked. After a while with the wine and conversation and hors d'oeuvres, Noreen forgot the little man and his deep-set eyes.

Until Daugherty asked her to dance and as they were approaching the floor, Noreen noticed that Athos was staring at them. Following her gaze, Daugherty stopped abruptly, canting his head slightly, as if in question. Athos nodded once and walked forward into the vessel.

"A bit of business," Daugherty explained, taking Noreen's arm and guiding her toward two men whom she knew and had earlier heard debating the engaging topic of the right time of year to get a mare with foal.

"William—d'you know Noreen Frenche?" Daugherty asked an older man with slicked-back, silver hair and a burgundy cummerbund. Except for a blond moustache as thick and trim as a brush, the man beside him could have been his twin. Both had passed up the exquisite champagne and were drinking whiskey.

"I should say I do. Would you believe we're contemporaries?"

"Where's Peter?" the other demanded. His eyes devolved on Daugherty, plainly not caring for what they saw.

"Then how about the proposition that I once had a crush on her mother that leaves me breathless still, when I remember."

"Up in Dublin is he? Long way from Dunlavin, this. Where's that blasted wog of a waiter?" Edward Hopper, a former T.D. and criminal lawyer, turned and imperiously summoned a steward.

Daugherty smiled quizzically—taken aback, she imagined, that she should know his acquaintances—then turned and hurried after Athos.

Noreen redirected the conversation to the topic she had heard them discussing earlier, and in a trice they were away at a gallop, debating the merits of how best to prepare a mare for stud. She only smiled politely and sipped at her champagne, while the two now quite old men firmed their stomachs and inflated their chests and strutted out their savvy of the activity which, as gentlemen, had given their lives point.

"Above all else, she should not look in any way neglected. I'm speaking—as Noreen will bear me out—of the mere matter of condition and care," the first, one William Crane, who was an old friend of her family, declaimed sonorously. "If turned out, she should be at least brushed over and looking cared for. Her feet should be properly trimmed and, of course, she should be unshod at least behind."

One of Hopper's legs moved involuntarily, as though re-experiencing some sight of a mare having kicked a stallion when he was most vulnerable.

"Then she should travel with a comfortable head collar that's clean and . . ." As the two old men prated on about appearances, Noreen asked herself how many times she had to listen to the very same, trivial subject discussed in, she believed, the very same words. And when—she glanced round the sumptuous and now crowded after-deck—had she last heard a new or interesting idea from these people? It was as though by conscious decision they had agreed, as a group, to limit their thoughts to a certain, acceptable set of subjects (horses, land, dogs, and sometimes cattle) and nearly everything else was ignored because it was tasteless. Then their commitment to tradition was so total that, she imagined, they could give reactionaryism a good name.

Hopper had rested two fingers on her wrist, and his large, whiskey-liquid eyes searched hers. " . . . every mare is an individual and should be treated as such in the way that suits her best. You know"—his eyes scanned the crowd, as though to include the gathering in his thought —"it all means a very great deal. Don't you agree?"

Noreen smiled, hating herself for the implied complicity and rethinking any—even the smallest—involvement with Daugherty. What would, what *could* life be like without Dublin with its dirt, decay, and endless differences? And a man who was unusual or surprising, at least in his thoughts. Her husband certainly was that. Always.

"The Hungarians have the best idea," said Hopper, his eyes still carefully regarding her; the last thing to be tolerated was a maverick and surely not a maverick mare. "It's a natural process and should have a natural, a time-honored, and an *acceptable*"—his shoe-brush moustache, which was still blond at the tips, twitched once—"genesis."

He meant the centuries-old practice in Hungary of allowing horses to roam free and form natural breeding herds of twenty to forty mares under a dominant stallion. The strong—or, rather, the genetically superior—animal survived to propagate, proponents such as Hopper contended, while the weak did not. Such a practice, however, ignored the several needs to which horses might be put and the fact that a good number of foals that would have died in unassisted births had grown to become champions. Weak or backward at birth did not necessarily mean weak or backward in life.

How far such an approach was, she mused, from all the estrus and breeding charts and the pedigree tables that covered a wall of Fionnuala Walton's office at Greenore Eugenics. Smiling at another man whom she believed she knew, hoping he would ask her to dance, she wondered what Hopper had meant by "acceptable" and what the purpose of that great table was. Certainly there had been a point. A breeding facility with such a reputation did not casually launch upon a forty-year experiment in planned husbandry without some goal. But what, given the seeming anomaly of the stallion, Taghmon, she could not guess.

Hunters and/or jumpers, she asked herself? Why, when there was little money in that and for the most part larger horses with great stamina and not quicker horses were required?

How capricious in comparison had been her own process of choosing a mate: a kiss followed by a slap in the office of her father's picture gallery, a barrage of flowers and presents, several dates, and an announcement that the product of at least three centuries of carefully planned eugenics (which had amounted to near in-breeding) would marry a short, squat, bald man twenty years her senior who was beset with at least two bad habits. Granted, officially sanctioned repressions and famines, the depredations of civil and other wars, and the pestilence of the slums had in regard at least to hardiness "perfected" his line, but her husband remained strictly a hybrid, if only on first viewing.

Was she, then, *naturally* attracted to Daugherty, who was intriguing in the manner of a well-bred stallion? In his features, his body, the way he carried himself, he appeared to be all one thing, as it were. But could she be *that* shallow?

And hadn't she felt the same way about her husband at one time? Did absence make the heart grow fonder, and was she missing her husband now? Or was it Daugherty she was missing and the temptation, which was hot, of having a "fling," as her unrelievedly silly friend had suggested? She glanced up at the moon. *Hot* was not exactly the word.

She was not being sensible, which was by everybody's account a salient characteristic of hers. And she knew herself (she now told herself) that any involvement with Daugherty, even the slightest and most "tangential," would change her marriage irrevocably. Her commitment would be breached, which would sicken her, and who knew then what would happen?

Her friend was a case in point. She had gone from fling to fling to affair after affair until now she—and not her tolerant husband—was contemplating divorce. She admitted her vows no longer meant anything to her, and she was burdened by guilt. She felt herself worthless. A tramp.

Granted Noreen was not the friend, but there was a certain lesson in that. Yet even after deciding that the friend's entire situation with those men was uncharacteristic and sleazy and that she needed psychiatric care, Noreen had found her thoughts returning again and again to the details of those assignations. What had it been like and how had she felt? How could it have been as passionate and as *violent* as the friend had related? And as the friend had said bluntly and others in subtle ways insinuated everyday, she herself was not getting any younger. Shortly her beauty would be gone. Could she be missing something that she would want when it was too late?

In refuge from her thoughts, she turned to the two men, whom she now decided she could not dislike. "Gentlemen—does either of you recognize the name Taghmon?"

"Certainly," said Hopper. It's an unremarkable village about ten miles due west."

"But no horse of that name?" she pressed.

Hopper's head went back.

Crane blinked several times rapidly, then said, "Now that you mention it I believe I do. Lovely-*looking* beast that showed some early promise but was brought along too fast, I hear, and went over the top. It was raced in France, I think. Owned by—" Crane then mentioned a stable, the trainer of which had a reputation for "burning" young mounts, and Hopper cleared his throat volubly, then looked away in disgust.

"The only reason I remember the animal is because Fi Walton, of all level-headed persons, paid nearly fifteen thousand quid for the nag at a bloodstock sale in Ballsbridge about—" He paused. "Four years ago at the spring sale," Hopper supplied. "Silly scene with some American —all money, no brains—bidding up the price beyond all value.

" 'What in the name of God could she'—Fi, I mean— 'want with the beast,' I can remember asking myself. People were actually calling out to her, 'Let it go. Let it go.' But she persisted and"—Crane finished his drink and glanced around for a steward.

"Could she have seen some promise in, say, the pedigree of the horse that others couldn't or didn't?"

Said Hopper, "Not likely. The punt had just begun to hit the skids, and the auction ring was packed with people on the make for a 'bargain,' as it were." By punt, he meant the Irish pound which in recent years had plummeted in value.

"Out of Madame Nora by Sunbury Prince, isn't he?" Crane asked.

Noreen nodded. "Nice conformation. A clay-colored bay with stockings to the cannons on all four legs."

Two pair of eyes fixed her. There was a pejorative pause during which Hopper glanced uncomfortably in the direction of Daugherty, who now stepped out of the shadow of the superstructure and approached them.

"The blaze and the cannons, surely," said Hopper. "But the horse was mahogany bay, if I'm not mistaken. As Eddy just said, it was . . . *is*, I should think, a handsome animal, if that sort of thing appeals to you. Deceiving, it is. Decidely."

"But why, then, would Miss Walton have launched upon an extensive breeding program with Taghmon?" Noreen, now utterly confused by the chart she had seen above the estrus tables in the Greenore Eugenics office, asked quickly.

111

Crane shook his head.

To him, Hopper said, "I've sworn off sexist gaffes, at least for this year." Savoring the deftness of the parry, he swung his eyes to Noreen.

By way of apology, Crane offered, "That's dry irony, in case it slipped by you. Like dry gin, it gives one a pain."

"What are we discussing here, horses?" asked Daugherty. And before either man could answer, he turned to Noreen. "Don't you find horses a rather dull and specialized subject?"

"No more so than, say, men," she replied. Over time, she imagined, his puerile insouciance could become as crashing a bore as Hopper's misogynism.

A line of doubt appeared on his brow. "You know something about horses?"

"Good God, man—I should say she does," Crane huffed. "Or at least she *should*. This is Noreen *Frenche*—"

"I was raised with horses," Noreen interrupted before the man could blurt out her married name."

"*Sam* Frenche's daughter?"

Said Hopper, "Is there another Frenche in horses in Ireland?"

Daugherty turned his eyes on her, and in them she read a genuine and warm if reckless regard (given Crane's and Hopper's presence) that again endeared him to her. "It gets better and better, and were you making fun of me, out there in the field this morning?" One dark eyebrow had arched playfully.

Crane looked away.

Hopper cleared his throat.

And hadn't it been her husband, after all, who had placed her here and in this role? Then why not then play it to the max? "We were, as I remember, speaking only of birds and bees and not of horses at all. Didn't you ask me to dance some minutes ago? Gentlemen, if you'll excuse us."

"Whoa," said Daugherty, winking to the other two men, as he followed her toward the orchestra.

And he was, as she had suspected, a good dancer—light on his feet, sure, but without any crass flamboyance. Strong, he pulled her into him and she could feel the girth of his chest. His hair was interestingly blond at the tips, either from the sun or some Viking blood in his genetic makeup, and as he turned her around and she saw Crane and Hopper following them with their eyes, she was filled with momentary anger at their presumption, which was based on a conception of human nature that was undoubtedly corrupt, if in some way accurate.

Where was the harm in learning more about herself and some others? Hadn't her life, as she had lived it, been too *good?* Could the feel of his hip against hers, his cheek on her temple, the way his work-hardened back devolved to a narrow waist be *bad?*

If only again to escape her thoughts as the music swelled to a crescendo, Noreen leaned away from him, the better to see his all-too-handsome face. Hadn't she decided already? Hadn't she concluded that it would change everything and not for the good? She had, but positioned like that, thigh to thigh, moving together, the vessel now rolling in a light swell, she again felt wild and foolish and dizzy.

She swung him around, her head tilted to the side, her eyes studying his features. "Tell me, sir, in twenty words or less—what are your hopes, dreams, and ambitions? And consider yourself flattered. It's the question I always ask of the men I'm about to devour." She swung him the other way.

Feigning fright, his eyes darted away at the others who

were leaning against the taffrail or sitting at the several tables there on the afterdeck. "In regard to what, your ladyship, and if you say women, sex, or love, I'll answer infinite to the first. To the second I'll say"—again his eyes strayed to the crowd, mostly, it seemed to allow her to scan the clean lines of his forehead, nose, and chin. With dark eyebrows and prominent, high cheekbones, he resembled some handsome bird of prey. "I dream of angular, red-haired, *married* women of taste, experience, and discretion with eyes the color of glacial ice though hearts like summer fire.

"My hopes? That some fine, summer night of a"—yet again he glanced away; she imagined it was a device that he had employed before and to effect— "full moon, say, at around five or—we'd best make it six—in the morning, such a goddess will choose to bestow her favors on me in —why not?—my mother's house, stealing down the hall past the dining room to the final door on the right and, like a succubus, into my room, which I leave unlocked for just such a possibility.

"And my ambitions?" Daugherty's dark eyes waited for hers to rise to them; the dance was drawing to a close. "Only to serve her well and true, such that in the morning she might, dare I say it? Are you ready?" He smiled wantonly and wickedly and—she judged—in just the manner that a married woman, who, like her silly friend, would allow herself and could engage in a fling would desire. "*Love* me as none other."

The music had stopped, and she was suddenly aware that they were alone on the dance floor, leaning into each other, their gazes locked. "How refreshingly different," she replied with a distance that masked rather well, she congratulated herself, the fact that on one level he still appealed to her very much. It only made the attraction annoyingly hotter. Like playing with the brightest flame, she wondered at the sear of his touch. It would be worse, she imagined, when he took her home. After the incident on the tractor, he would try there, she knew. And would she—*could she*—hold out?

"I feared that there was not a man here who would not have mentioned horses, when asked that question. Our host excluded, of course. For him, it's probably ships." Or death, she thought, seeing Athos again watching them, as she broke from Daugherty and turned to where she thought the bar had been. A stiff, calming drink would do her good; her emotions had not done such battle with her sense in years. Nor would they probably again, she reminded herself once more.

"You're wrong there," Daugherty said after she had been served another glass of champagne; he himself refused the steward's offer.

"About what?"

"About Athos. He rather fancies the odd nag, and he's willing to pay, it seems."

"Is that why you abandoned me so abruptly to the care of Rosinante and Sleipnir?" She meant Crane and Hopper, and in raising the glass, Noreen glanced round to see who else might have been staring at them. More than a few were still watching, and she was sure the gossip would reach Dublin before she could return. It was endemic to the country, and any indiscretion in the tender of the public eye raged, like fire in wind.

"My second choice."

"Your second choice in regard to what?"

Hopper now cleared his throat volubly. His face was red, no doubt from drink, and he shivered his jowls in demonstrable disapproval, before turning his back to them and looking out to sea.

"Hopes, dreams, and ambitions, of course. Or are you interested only in the *essential* me?"

Taking his arm, she drew him out of the direct light and into the shadow of the canopy near the taffrail. A breeze that was strong in gusts but still warm had sprung up. Slowly the yacht had begun to swing round on its anchor. The tide was turning. "Yes and no," she replied flirtatiously, letting him feel the full effect of her eyes, now that she believed she had gained some hold of herself. "Since I suspect you'll only tell me of some super horse."

Daugherty's features darkened somewhat. "Why do you say that?"

"Isn't it every breeder's dream? Or is yours somehow" —she paused, smiling in a way that she hope would goad him—"different?"

He cocked his head in a gesture which that morning she had seen his mother employ. It was as though he were listening to some interior voice. He then looked up and smiled. "Certainly it's different. Categorically. It's a difference in—"

"Kind," she supplied. She shook her head slightly and sipped from the glass. "An old story. No, Mr. Daugherty —you're a pleasant man, but no different from the standard, strong, handsome, desirable horse breeder."

"Think you not?"

She smirked deprecatingly and looked away. "It's not a matter for thought."

Daugherty folded his arms across his chest, and, half-sitting on the rail, moved closer to her. Staring out at the others, some of whom had begun to dance again, he said in a confidential but still playful tone, "I'm right in assuming that you know *something* about thoroughbreds?"

As he had only moments before, she now inclined her head to one side. "Somehow I think the man is about to

116

confide in me. Shall I warn him I'm a notorious snitch?"

But without responding to the jest, Daugherty continued on, "And as a breed their perfection has more or less peaked—in configuration, the relationship of muscle mass to body weight, lung capacity, heart size, pulse rate. Performance in every sort of test—on the flat, over hurdles, steeplechase, three-day eventing, you name it, has plateaued off.

"But what would you have," he said in a voice so low that she had to strain to hear, "what would you have *if,* through some burst of genetic insight, you found you could take formerly denigrated horses with poor pedigrees and even poorer performance records and breed a line of super-sires?"

"Another Federico Tessio." Noreen touched the glass to her lips and made sure her eyes sparkled with supposed humor. Tessio was the now legendary breeder who had taken no-account horses, like Pharos and Nogara, and created Nearco who was the sire of Nasrullah, grandsire of Bold Ruler, and founder of the sire line that produced Native Dancer.

"No, no—seriously." He had moved yet closer to her, and his tone was suddenly more than simply serious. He was speaking of a passion and of—she was now certain—the chart she had seen on the wall in the office. "What would you have?"

As though it was still a matter of little interest, she replied, "Perhaps one spectacular horse. You must remember that, unlike the blood of the great majority of stallions, Nearco's blood proved extraordinarily prepotent." She meant that the get produced by Nearco more closely resembled its sire than its dam and was able to pass the traits derived from its patrimony along to its own get.

Daugherty smiled and looked away. "What if you could be sure of that as well?"

Noreen tried not to frown. There was no way to be sure that traits such as speed and stamina had been passed to the offspring apart from testing them against other horses, and certainly the world would be aware of the results.

As if unconcerned, she placed her elbows on the rail and leaned back. She glanced up at him slowly, languorously, knowing the effect her green eyes could have. She then scanned the crowd, catching sight of Crane and Hopper, who were leaving. She did not have to guess what they would say about Daugherty's—was it claim?—though she herself had viewed a horse at Greenore Eugenics that had seemed very fair indeed. "Is that what you and Fionnuala Walton are up to at Greenore Eugenics?"

Daugherty's forehead tightened, his ears pulled back. He studied her face. "What makes you ask that?"

"Her specialty is genetics, is it not? University trained, as I remember her telling me when last we met. How is she, bye the bye? I haven't seen her . . . well, since I myself was in school. Should I stop by? Is she busy?"

Daugherty took her arm. "Come. It's time to leave. And there're your friends, Hopper and Crane, thanking Nicky for the gargle. We must let them see that we're not chaperoned."

And at the Mercedes on the jetty, Daugherty had scarcely opened the door before he said, "The chauffeur will see you home. I didn't want to tell you earlier and ruin the evening, but another little thing has come up. I don't know when I'll be back. Dawn, perhaps later. Keep that bed warm." He then leaned into the car and, wrapping his arm around the small of her back, lifted her up into him. He then kissed her full on the mouth, long and hard and with a kind of ferocity that left her breathless.

"I don't understand."

He flicked up his chin, as though to humor a slow child or, worse, a dumb woman. "What don't you understand?"

"Little *thing?*" It was, she would later think, one of those difficult moments in life, when the disjunction between the thought stated and the thought received proved a painful, irremediable embarrassment that would make her blush whenever she remembered: that though she herself had in fact decided to spurn his advances, she thought by "little thing" he had meant some other woman. And then the confident gall of his supposing that she and he had already agreed on what would follow without—

He chuckled triumphantly. "Don't you worry, now. You're my heart's desire, and I'll be back soon. Another 'nagging' bit of business down at Carnsore Point, which is what will take the time." And did she even see him smile in the shadow of the door? She thought she did. "Remember now. Last door past the dining room. Mind that you mess up your bed. Mither has a touch of Sherlock, she has. And she records every little transgression, no matter how slight. For 'the edge,' as she says."

"Fear not—I won't be too tired.

"The farm, Sean," said Daugherty, and before she could respond, the door was closed and the car moved off with Noreen stunned and wondering at the change. Had it been her allusion to Fionnuala Walton that had cooled him on her presence? It was not quite the best word. Or had it—as she assumed he had implied—something to do with Athos and whatever discussion they had had on the yacht? Or had it been something else about which she didn't and couldn't know?

In any case, she felt—was it rejected? It was, and—as the Mercedes climbed Greenore Point and she looked out at the harbor lights and bit into a knuckle—angry. Very angry indeed.

Had she in fact thrown herself at him? She glanced down at the sheer silk of her evening gown and assumed that, whereas she *knew* she really *hadn't*, the galling part was that he obviously thought she had.

How else to explain the presumption of his, "Don't worry now, you're my heart's desire," and his, "Mind that you mess up your bed," and finally the unmitigated arrogance of, "Fear not—I won't be too tired."

"Janie Mack!" she kept herself from shouting at the roof of the car. "The egotist! The wretch!"

Well, whatever it was that had kept him from divulging the fact of Fionnuala Walton's murder and the nature of his "bits" of business with Athos and, now, back at Carnsore Point in the dead of night, she would find out.

It was in some way involved, she now told herself, with the murder. Or at least she hoped it was.

Without pausing to change her clothes, Noreen waited inside the front door of the Daugherty house, listening for the Mercedes to move off. There was a wind up, which was wailing in the distance toward the north and the head land.

She thought of her husband and how he would prefer to know about her suspicions (could they be more than that?) as soon as possible. Taking her pocket secretary from her purse, she held the scratch pad into the shaft of dim light that was falling through the entry transom and quickly noted the main points of what she had learned:

Taghmon's chart in the Eugenics' office; what she had read of the horse in the *Stud Book;* Daugherty's description of the breeding experiment as an attempt to sire a line of "super horses"; his meeting with Athos aboard the

Amphitrite; and finally the other planned meeting with somebody out on Carnsore Point.

Placing the note in an envelope that contained a gas bill, she crossed out their Rathmines address and wrote, "c/o Binn na Rinn Farms, Greenore Point, County Wexford." She licked the glued edge and tried to get it to hold. Only one side of the flap stuck. She thought of the mother, Mna, and how inquisitive she seemed. Would she open it and read the note? If so, would she be able to guess who it was from?

Noreen decided to take the chance that she wouldn't even look into the envelope, McGarr being with the Gárda and all. She placed it in the mailbox that hung from the interior side of the door, then eased the door open and stole across the gravel drive toward her Deux Chevaux, which she could just see in the deep shadows beneath the chestnut trees.

8

The same mournful keening that Noreen heard across the fields had awakened McGarr an hour earlier. At first he too mistook it for the wind, as slowly, painfully, still sitting in the armchair where he had nodded off, he collected his thoughts and roused himself.

But unlike the wind in any of its moods, it was both a plaintive sound, like a chorus of newborn babes crying for succor or kittens mewing for milk, and savagely shrill—baleful and atavistic—with an intent that was undisguisedly hostile. In one way it reminded him of the upper register of the chanter of a bagpipe, playing some wild, ancient lament, half curse. In another it was so grating, so insistent and ugly, that it demanded to be dealt with, and now.

And why now? he asked himself as he straightened up from a basin of cold water in which he had doused his face. Deirdre and Dan? What was the point of what, listening closely before he placed the towel on its holder, he could only consider a kind of attack? For it was a stigma that would be remembered and remarked on for the rest of their lives. Something in their pasts? Some flaw? Some crime?

Switching out the light and opening a window wide, McGarr listened for the direction of the wailing. With only a sense that its source lay somewhere off to the east and perhaps the north, McGarr slipped out of the window and eased himself down onto the thick slates that functioned as a splash guard around the periphery of the old farmhouse. He paused only at Mna Daugherty's bedroom.

She was sitting in a tall rocker with a floor lamp on one side and a small, battered table on the other. She had a large ledger book in one hand and the receiver of a telephone in the other. Still wearing the plain black dress, she had pushed her eyeglasses down on her nose and with eyes closed was smiling slightly, as she listened.

After a while, she said, "Me? Now why would I want to go and do that? It's just some of the lads poking a bit of fun, is all, and you should take it in the spirit it's given." She listened further, her smile growing wider. Without opening her eyes, she reached for the glass and took a long, obviously satisfying swallow. She turned to the side and laughed silently, placing the glass back on the table.

"Sure, I always said, what's good for the horses and cattle must have some application to family life. I'm only after telling one of yous that I want a bit for me own and look what happened to her. Tomorrow would be as good a time as any to patch things up."

Her eyes then opened and she held the receiver away, then uttering a small chortle of satisfaction, placed it carefully in its yoke. She again reached for the glass, and McGarr, buffeted with a gust laden with that special sound, hurried on.

It was an unusual summer night, warm and mellow, with a sky so high and lucid that it looked slick, like wet, inky lacquer on which chips of gemstones had been sprayed. Yet from the sea to the north and east, dense patches of cloud with ragged white edges were driving in low, blinding the face of the nearly full moon, plunging the land into occasional darkness.

With a tug at the brim of his cap, McGarr leaned into the gusty summer wind and lurched up the avenue of chestnuts that were rocking above him, the limbs black arms on the midnight-blue sky. Pausing now and again to listen, he determined at length that the wailing was coming from the direction of Greenore House, and he broke into a trot that after a painful hundred yards banished his aches and made the blood pound in his temples. Then suddenly, peremptorily, a cloud passed across the moon, and the land was plunged into darkness. He had to walk —grope—toward the sound, taking tall steps to keep from falling over any stone in the dirt road.

But the wailing continued, and finding by feel the hedges and gate, McGarr tapped with his toe the slates of the walkway. The first, the second. He then moved purposefully forward and in close—he believed—to the house, when the off-round headlamp of the moon glared out from behind a cloud bank and left him blinking up at the crisp, gabled outline of the Edwardian structure, which was silhouetted on the lighter sky.

"Nary a hair or you're dead," a woman's voice ordered, and the beam of a pocket torch was snapped on to illuminate one of the Walton sisters—the older one, Siobhan— sitting on the front stairs, both hands on some great, long-barreled, sporting gun that was pointed at McGarr's chest.

The light then swung round and flashed in his eyes, and the wailing, which had stopped for a moment, began again: a single note, high and shrill and oscillating and followed by a chorus of others from where? McGarr spun around and thought he saw a figure dip below the hedge there to the south.

It was then that the gun went off, a blast that rocked McGarr and passed a searing heat across the side of his face. He went down from caution and fright, then launched himself off his heels at the woman, who became two, above him—hacking and scratching at him—and his hand felt the hot double barrel, which he jerked up.

It discharged again and jarred him from his fist right down to his toes. He tugged once, then twice, then seizing the barrel with both hands wrenched it from their grasp and hurled it out onto the lawn.

"Why?" he demanded.

"Why *what?*" another voice, which he recognized as that of the second sister, Machala, answered.

"Why the gun? You could have killed somebody. And why the . . ." He turned to the shrieking, which had begun again, and now seemed to him derisive, as though a kind of hideous, cruel fun were being poked at him.

"Because of your niece?" he asked when neither answered. "Well—come closer while I tell yah"—he blurted out, his anger swelling with the wind and the blowing that now seemed to come at them from every side of the hedges—"she's up to her neck in your sister's murder, and you'll have some answers for me, you will, on the morrow."

McGarr pivoted and passed his eyes across the line of the hedge. Catching sight of what looked like a head bob up, he sprinted low, keeping his head down so he would —like them—not be seen. They knew why they were blowing, and an answer he would get.

But as he hurled himself over the hedges, a cloud moved across the moon, and he fell onto at least two bodies in a darkness that allowed them to pull themselves free and blunder off.

"What was that?" a voice perhaps fifteen yards away whispered.

"Nuttin'," said McGarr in the same tone, trying to place its direction as he gathered himself into another crouch. "I fell is all." But when he approached the locus of the voice and lunged forward, he caught only a painful heel in the shoulder.

The moon then reappeared, and he saw what seemed like shadows or wraiths, flitting over the rolling grassland to the south. Boys, they were, whom McGarr would never catch. The "lads," and probably not out of their teens. One thing was plain, however—they were too young to have gotten the idea on their own. Somebody had put them up to it, and McGarr remembered Mna Daugherty's voice on the phone.

And instead of returning to the sisters and their long gun, he followed at a fast walk the southward sweep of the blowers over the moonlit fields. He had to wait when the moon was obscured until, after a long pause of darkness, he heard the wailing again. Moving toward it, he topped the crest of a hill and looked down on an array of lights in a collection of buildings below him.

Horse barns, they were, with large, metal-sheathed out-buildings and paddock areas, and a well-kept track ring-ing all. One barn in the middle was more brightly lit than the others and there, it seemed, the blowers had gath-ered.

With resolution now—knowing they would see him, knowing they would scatter—McGarr moved down into the basin, keeping his eyes on the lighted windows where, as he approached, he could see a woman, the niece, seated a few feet inside the open door on a stool by a tall, closed stable box.

Dan Daugherty Jr., her fiancé, was looming above her, his great size casting a shadow into which McGarr now stepped.

She had lowered her head to her forearms, which she had wrapped about her knees. Her ponytail had swung to one side to expose her neck. In the harsh light from bright bulbs set high on the barrel ceiling of what amounted to a long Nissen hut, her neck was thin and ivory. She was, he assumed from the way her body rocked, sobbing.

". . . but we must," she was saying through her tears. "We've got no choice but to give over."

"And g-give up w-what could provide for us a v-veritable—" There was a painful pause filled by wailing so close to the windows that the horses began to panic. They whinnied and reared, some kicking the sides of their boxes. "—dynasty on the track?" Daugherty completed. "F-Fi and Dan, my father—they p-planned for this. After he got s-sick, it was the one b-big b-b-break G-Greenore Eugenics a-always needed and never g-got. To th-throw it away would just—"

"But he's got the stallion. He could have the papers too. And now this"—she looked up toward the door and the darkness and the blowing and saw McGarr. Her head went back, her mouth dropped open.

Daugherty wheeled around. As though in reflex, one hand grabbed for McGarr's lapel, while the other formed a fist.

Rearing yet farther back, he delivered a blow that instead glanced off McGarr's shoulder, as the latter dropped to his knees and jerked down on the extended left arm. Hurtling forward with the momentum of the punch, the man fell roughly into the dirt. McGarr brushed off his knees and began to step into the barn, as the wailing continued. A few of the blowers now chanced to reveal themselves at the windows.

But with surprising speed for a big man, Daugherty soon gained his feet. Muttering to himself, he soon appeared before McGarr.

"Stay out!" He roared and blinked, as though surprised himself at the clarity of the statement. Again his large left hand was extended, his right fist cocked.

McGarr only made to step in one direction and, when the man committed himself to stopping him there, he moved quickly past him on the other side.

The girl had raised her head.

A hand then fell roughly on McGarr's shoulder and spun him around.

"Now—I want you to stop," McGarr said into Daugherty's clenched-jaw grimace, as the young man roared something unintelligible and aimed another blow at his head.

"You're playing the fool here." McGarr grabbed the left arm, spun Daugherty around and jerked it up behind his back. Placing his foot on the small of the man's back, he then thrust him back out into the darkness where he again fell.

The wailing had stopped, and McGarr could now hear laughter. He stepped toward the niece. "Just the woman I wanted to see. Is there somewhere we can talk in private?" He yet again heard the shuffle of feet behind him. "Away from"—he turned to see Daugherty in the doorway of the stable, his fists clenched by his side, his eyes like two red pokers—"your man, and I'll tell you this but once. I'm tired of him, and I want you to make him stop before he's hurt. As it is, I could have you up on charges."

And did he see her smirk before her eyes strayed to the faces in the windows? He did, though he had little time to study her.

Hands that pinned his arms to his sides with such force that he could not move lifted McGarr bodily off his feet. He was spun around and rushed past the closed doors of the tall birthing stall toward the other side of the stable and a recessed area which was heaped with piles of muck.

There a half-dozen pitchforks, maybe more, had been placed in a rack, prongs up, and, rushing McGarr forward, Daugherty groaned with an enormous effort and hurled McGarr toward them.

He had time only to push out with his bare hands in an attempt to knock away the shiny barbs.

With a whistle and a pop, one skidded up the surface of his windbreaker and pierced the material, just missing his left bicep. Another lay cold, where he had fallen on the rack, against his neck. The others, it seemed, had all missed him, until he tried to raise himself up.

He could not move his right hand. Through it completely, like a single, silver fang, a prong had slipped, yet curiously he had not felt the wound nor did it now hurt. It was more numb or hot or tingling, though when he tried to wrench himself free, he found his hand, like a plank impaled on a long spike.

And Daugherty, who had stumbled, was now picking himself up. Turning to him, McGarr believed he had seen eyes like that before—glassy with rage, eyes that had lost contact with reality and could and would kill.

McGarr jerked the hand. He flailed it from side to side, the pain now a searing flash up his arm to his neck, his face and his head.

And Daugherty, who had gained his feet, had something in his hand—long and heavy, which with an effort he now swung back over his head and lurched forward. A tractor apparatus pin, a kind of weighted pry bar, McGarr saw, as with a curious distraction he turned to watch.

Yet without having to think, McGarr reached with his free hand into the welter of tines and snatched up one of the pitchforks beside him. Trying to turn to face him, he hurled it at Daugherty. And another and another, until the young man, bellowing his anger and sidestepping each, moved behind him. It was only then that McGarr confronted his pain.

Using the space that he had cleared on top of the rack, he swiveled the impaled hand around on the galling prong and—again with the other hand—tugged it up the length of shiny barb. He then threw himself back just as the pry bar whistled past his head and shivered the frame of the rack, knocking him back into the shadows and sending the remaining pitchforks clattering across the concrete.

Daugherty had stumbled, and in the pause in which both men picked themselves up, McGarr considered the depths of his own anger that was now profound and directed mainly at himself.

Yes—it was now painfully clear to him that his holiday was over, and he doubted at the moment if he would ever allow himself to take another. For—*yes*—he had been remiss in not summoning his entire squad the moment he had understood that Fionnuala Walton's death had not been accidental. And—*yes again*—he had been wrong to dawdle along with the investigation in a kind of pleasurable limbo, tasting the evidence—like the liquor, which at the behest of others he had quit—instead of cleaving to his own practices, which had proved themselves in the past at least protective of his person.

After all—it occurred to him, as he shook the blood from the injured hand and tried to make a fist—the crime had been murder, and the stakes were more than simply high. There was the matter of his wife. What could he have been thinking of to have "invited" her (could that be what had happened in the name of sharing time together?) to the farm of the mother of the man before him? He could not relieve her of that burden soon enough, he now believed. And where was she? Why hadn't she returned from that party with the brother by the time McGarr had awakened, which had been when? He couldn't remember. He had scarcely given her a thought.

And finally, there was the girl, the niece, whom he should have legally detained the moment he knew that the prints on the farrier's claw were—like the shoe print in the dust behind the door—hers. She, who was now standing above in the stable area looking down at them, had something to tell him. And she would, he vowed as he neared Daugherty, whose open hands were poised as though he would lunge and soon.

The hand, the injured one, could not make a fist, but it was bloody, a show, and the fingers could point.

McGarr now circled Daugherty, whom he had mistaken as—what had been the mother's term?—"afflicted" and therefore harmless. But what else did he know of him? That he was, in fact, university-trained, a poet like the father, and then the fiancé of a woman who might soon inherit most of Greenore Point, a going concern, and —who knew?—other assets as well. Young Daugherty could soon find himself a wealthy—doubtless the wealthiest—man in those parts.

Conclusion? He was a lucky or devious and most certainly a dangerous man. McGarr remembered how he had kept the niece from changing the condition of the farrier's claw, how he had drawn her away from the scene before she could commit a blunder. And what else had the mother said about him? "He'd have the world in his pocket, could he but make it jump." McGarr wondered if he considered murder the essential leap.

McGarr held up the hand that was now sticky with blood. "Guess what?" he said. "Doesn't hurt a bit. Really. Must've passed right through some spot with no nerves." Although now nearly within Daugherty's reach, McGarr, smiling quizzically, had turned his attention to the hand. He felt as he had when in his youth in Inchicore, then perhaps the worst of Dublin's several slums, he had had to take on the neighborhood bully or a thief or, more than a few times, a man. And he would suffer no mere farm boy, no matter how large or strong, to mess him about with impunity.

Daugherty's hands were now within inches of him, he judged. "There's blood, sure."

Daugherty took another small step, his body tensing.

"And the hole—" McGarr turned the hand over and then flipped it back. "—as you can see yourself, it's like it's already healed."

The gaze quavered toward the hand just the little bit that McGarr was watching for, and two bloody fingers shot out and buried themselves deep in Daugherty's eyes.

While from as low as he could in one motion reach, McGarr loaded every ounce of his weight into the fist of his right hand and a punch that snapped—he could feel it—Daugherty's sternum and drove the breath from his lungs. Another blow far lower caused the large man to double over. And yet another—a rocking uppercut— nearly bent him in two.

With the injured hand that twitched with every throb of his pulse, McGarr grabbed a fistful of Daugherty's wavy black hair and snapped up his head.

"Pretty, isn't it, this face?" he asked in the same quizzical tone he had used to examine the hand. "It's the nose, it is," he went on. "Seldom see one like that. Straight. No curve up, no curve down. Surely no bend to the side. No flattening. No breaks."

Daugherty was out on his feet. Both hands were plunged between his legs. His eyes had sunk back into his head. There was a fleck at one corner of his mouth that McGarr guessed was vomit. But yet he managed to move in a long, retreating stumble—back out into the stable area toward the open door and the darkness beyond.

McGarr swung his head to the stable area, but she was gone, and from behind him—on the side of his neck, his face and his head—the blow fell. And again and again, knocking him to the side and away from Daugherty, driving him down on one knee until the good hand came up and caught and held whatever was striking him.

A heavy chunk of oaken frame from the shattered rack, which he jerked away and hurled toward the stable.

But she was then upon him, the niece, hacking and scratching. "You bloody bastard," she enunciated with a precision that was not native. "You low, craven wretch," as he tried to focus through bursts of phosphorescent pain that now muted through the spectrum to a deep, purple rage, mostly at himself. He had made another, gross error in having forgotten her. His face—he could now feel it again—was running with blood.

With a shrug and a push he threw her off, and the back of his good hand shot out at where, he suspected, she was. It caught her hard—it cracked—on the side of her face, just once. And then there was a silence that lasted a few seconds, while McGarr searched through the waves of color, which were continuing, and his blood to find her on the floor.

Said some playful, distant voice, "Look out, now. She's got a fork."

And only as McGarr's sight cleared and he stepped to the side and she rushed past him did he realize he had not heard or was not hearing the blowing.

He had to reach, to lunge for her, and his hand snagged in her hair, the ponytail. Pivoting blindly but with no little vehemence, he swung the side of his right foot and caught her in back of her knees, taking her legs out from under her. Caught by her hair, she fell roughly to the concrete. "You son of a bitch, you'll pay for this."

But with a face now in every window, McGarr began pulling her by her ponytail through the manure toward the stable area, her hands now clasped on his, the nails digging in, gouging.

"No, not there!" she shouted, as he dragged her toward the box before which was gathered a small cot, two stools, and a cooler. "It's only a mare with foal. She's ill. You'll kill them. Let me up!"

But McGarr slid the bolt nonetheless, and looked upon a huge, red mare truculent from the niece's shrieking and all the noise before. Behind her was a younger horse.

In a small room, the door of which was perhaps twenty feet distant, McGarr discovered another cot and a rack hung with clothes that were obviously Daugherty's. With force so that she cried out, he skidded her across the floor and into a wall.

Bending to her as, truly terrified, she now tried to escape, pushing herself down the wall, McGarr showed her the back of his hand, the one she had scraped raw. "That's you," he flicked his wrist, slapping her face hard. He raised the other hand. "That's your man." He slapped her sharply again. "And this is justice and something, I suspect, you should have gotten years ago." The third slap rocked her head.

Her strange, ultramarine-colored eyes were running with tears, her cheeks were bright red.

"Now for the questions and I warn you—even the hint of a lie and I'll beat you bloody. Why did I find your fingerprints on that farrier's claw?"

McGarr waited, hoping that shock and not intransigence was the cause of her silence. He did not want to have to strike her again, but he would. It was police work at its rawest.

But when he raised a hand to wipe the blood from his eyebrow, she flinched and blurted out, "I found it there on the floor in the attic, after I found my aunt and phoned the police."

When McGarr still said nothing, she blinked and lowered her head and tears not of anger but of—he judged —relief began. She sobbed, "I saw the light and I went up. Fi kept the key to the attic herself, and I'd only known her to open it once before . . . after Uncle Dan . . . I mean, Dan Daugherty died."

McGarr eased back on his heels and tried to find a way of holding the hand that would ease the pain. He took another tug on the flask.

"I saw it there on the floor."

"Where on the floor?"

"Right in the middle of the attic floor. Between the trunks. Almost as if it had been . . . placed there, I later thought. But then, well, I assumed immediately that it had been Dan, my fiancé, who—" There was a pause; she had said "immeedjitly."

"Who *what?*"

"Who had murdered her."

"Why *murder?*"

She looked away, then lifted the waistband of a black turtleneck jumper and pulled a frilly, flowered handkerchief from under the belt of her riding trousers. Her skin there was very dark, as if she had been sunbathing regularly or had passed the winter in a warmer clime.

"Aunt Fi was a most careful person and in her own right, apart from the breeding and all, a sportswoman. And fit. Why—up until the day she died people mistook her for being only in her forties. Even Tommy thought—" She glanced up at McGarr. "—but that's gossip."

"I'll hear it."

She wagged her head, as though distressed. With those eyes, her oval face and dark features, she was an unusually attractive woman, McGarr judged. He looked away, as she blew her nose.

The wailing had not begun again, and McGarr wondered why—fear and pity, the hour which for schoolboys was late, or simply because they had made their point. Carefully McGarr eased back the bloody cuff of his windbreaker to check his watch. It was broken, smashed. He guessed it was about two o'clock.

"It's no secret that Fi had taken Tom as her lover long before his father died. Years ago when I was only a young girl and he came back from the riding he'd been doing in England and elsewhere. Fi was, you know, a 'liberated' woman, and she liked her men."

"But why did you think Dan—your Dan"— McGarr swung his head to the door, only now remembering that he might reappear, —"might have murdered her?"

"Well—he has a temper, as you've seen for yourself." The eyes rose to his, then shied to his hand which he was holding up to ease the pain and lessen the bleeding.

"And she was objecting to your marriage?" he asked,

trying to mask his incredulity. It was the last position, he imagined, that she who was herself childless and had been so intimately involved with the Daughertys would have adopted.

"After her talk with Dan's mother."

"Mna?" McGarr had heard what the Daugherty woman had said she had discussed with the victim—the property and the "dowry," which had seemed to him odd and merely the attempt of a crafty, countrywoman to gain the last little advantage from a neighbor. "What could she have possibly said to your aunt to make her object?"

"Dan's wildness. His . . . immaturity, I guess, but, you know, he's not like that at all underneath. First honors, mind you, up at Trinity. He could think rings around the others. There."

And here as well, McGarr wondered, considering the startlingly handsome woman before him and what might likely be her fortune?

"But I saw the tool and the way it seemed like she'd been . . . flung or had . . . dived down the stairs. The runner"—she sobbed—"there at the top of the stairs had never been loose, and how could it have become so with the attic never used?

"I picked it up, like this"—she raised her index finger and her thumb—"and tried to place it back on the peg where it belonged behind the door. But I lacked the height to do it properly, and then, later, after having seen my footprint there in the dust, it occurred to me how *arranged* it all seemed. It was as though somebody had actually wanted me or somebody else to discover the tool and handle it and then step there behind the door."

"Later?"

"Yes—after you and Superintendent Stack had left, I

went up to—well, to wipe off what I knew must be my fingerprints."

"Alone?"

"Yes, though Dan found me there and prevented me from making what would have been a blunder."

She was not lying, McGarr concluded, at least about that. "Properly?" he asked.

A furrow appeared on the smooth line of her brow.

"Your not being able to hang the tool *properly?*"

"The way it was supposed to attach."

"But hadn't you only been up there once before?"

"Yes, but it was like a revelation, that attic. There all along I'd thought she'd been very much the professional woman, the woman of science and reason, and her need for men had been a 'physiological necessity,' as she had once phrased it after I'd walked in on her and Tom in the tack room. She told me it had been Dan—the father— who had encouraged her to take Tommy to her bed. 'Why, sure—don't look so shocked,' she said. 'In the best breeding circles it's done.'

"But there she'd compiled the most maudlinly romantic journals and not merely in her youth. There was one for every year of her life right up—I'd be willing to bet— to yesterday," she looked away, "if she had the chance. She'd even saved the tools Dan Senior had used when serving with the British Army."

"Then she didn't object to your sleeping here?" McGarr chanced.

The eyes blinked. The finely shaped arch of her nostrils pulsed. "On the contrary—she encouraged me to. 'Ovulations,' she once said. 'Make sure you bed him when you're ovulating. With the Daughertys it's children that count. Blood and their clan, and don't to your sorrow forget.' "

"And you're her heir?"

"She once told me as much."

"To—?"

" 'All I possess,' she said. 'Divisions only weaken a line. It's the purity of transference, generation to generation, that confers strength.' "

McGarr was rather amazed at how specific her memory was of her aunt's thoughts, but then so many seemed to touch her life directly. "And she possessed?"

"The house, the property, the business, and then a number of investments that she and her father before her made. They total several millions of pounds sterling and are controlled by trust through a London investment house. Fi showed me the portfolio, oh"—the eyes glanced up at the ceiling—"a year ago, perhaps longer. Dan, my Dan, checked the day after she died, which gives you an idea of his 'immaturity.' "

"You're pregnant?" McGarr again hazarded.

She smiled slightly. "Happily." Turning her head to the side, she reached up with a finger and smoothed a strand of wavy, dark hair that had strayed onto her forehead. In that light her resemblance to her fiancé was marked, though it had been McGarr's experience to note that couples often shared some physical similarity. It was a matter of ego, he supposed. He considered his own wife who shared with him only what had once been his red hair.

"I hope your treatment of me just now hasn't altered my condition."

Not likely, thought McGarr. In that hard, diminutive body there was steel. "And where were you at the time?"

"Of what?"

"Of the murder, of course? Your Aunt Siobhan tells me you'd retired for a nap." With difficulty McGarr stood and made his way toward a small basin.

"I had." She touched a hand to her stomach. "I mean,

139

I had begun to go up, but I met Fi on the stairs. She asked me to pop into Kilranell to fetch some supplies Siobhan had told her she absolutely needed at that moment or supper would be a bomb. A fool's errand I knew then, as I know now. She had mentioned perhaps a week before that she wanted to have it out with Mna, once and for all."

"*What* out?" McGarr stretched his palm as completely as he could with the swelling. Into the puncture, which now opened, he poured some whiskey that pooled there. He awaited the burn.

"Everything—about the property, Dan, Tommy, Danny, and to claim victory."

"She told you that?" McGarr managed to say.

"Not in so many words, but she didn't have to say it. This isn't Dublin."

Lamentably, thought McGarr, his feet wanting to dance with the sting. He thought of the pitchfork and the manure wallow. Cleansing that wound would not be so easy or painless.

"One tends to know a great deal about the few people she encounters in such a setting," she went on in a didactic tone.

McGarr wondered if she thought he resided on Mars or, worse, in Dublin. "Then why the blowing," he asked, bending his head to the cool, soothing water that now sluiced over his hands. He touched some to his now scabbing pate. It would be weeks before he looked and felt right.

"Mna's behind that, I'm sure."

"But how?" At the small basin that the room contained, McGarr applied some soap to his face and then to the top of his head. He held the injured hand by his side. "Money?" They both knew that would not be enough to have the blowers turn against Dan and her. First, the charge against the woman before him and her fiancé would have to be fair and provable. Only then would some further inducement be acceptable.

"All I can think of is some news of the murder, some word passed in the right place. Money or the promise of a job."

Gossip again, he thought. Then why no press? "Speak to anybody about your aunt?"

She shook her head. She was watching him closely as he moved toward the door.

"Butcher, greengrocer. Somebody who works here?"

"I haven't been out. Tommy suspended operations. Told the staff to take a short holiday."

So McGarr had learned on the phone. "On what excuse?"

"Inventory, though he might have done better. Confidence—in the product but as much in the breeder and her rectitude—is essential in this business. And trust. You can't expect people to splash out tens of thousands, sometimes hundreds of thousands of pounds on the say-so of people who are involved in a murder. It would be death to the business." Her eyes darted away from McGarr.

"And that's the reason I haven't read a word of your aunt in the press? That nobody—no groom, no official of the firm, no Daugherty or Walton—wants to lose his job, that everybody could keep himself or," he made sure their eyes met, "herself from mentioning it?

"There's to be a wake, I suppose?"

She shook her head. "Auntie wouldn't have wanted it."

McGarr glanced down at his shoes, which also were ruined. "A funeral?"

"Well, yes. But—"

"A simple ceremony," McGarr interposed. "Just family and a few old friends. No, maybe no old friends, who tend to gossip. Just family and more family, you know, the *big* family. By that I mean the Daughertys too. Will the mother be invited?"

"Mna?" the niece asked. "You should know that early yesterday morning she filed an agreement with the courts to purchase a large part of Greenore Eugenics property. The note must have been signed at her meeting with Fi. Mna also ordered her solicitor to petition the courts to have Fi's will read before any inquest."

Towel in hand, McGarr glanced up. "Grounds?"

"That the settlement of the estate is crucial to the functioning of the two concerns and vital to the economy of Southeast Wexford, or some such truck. Greenore Eugenics *and* Binn na Rinn Farms, she means."

"When?"

"Tomorrow at eleven in court chambers, Wexford Town."

"Before the funeral."

She looked away. A sentimental group, thought McGarr. He wondered if the pathologist was even through with the victim or if anybody cared. Then he rather marveled at how fast Mna Daugherty had moved and how quickly *that* news had traveled.

He patted dry the wounds on top of his head, then wrapped the towel round his hand.

He went out to look for his cap.

9

Noreen parked the Deux Chevaux beyond Churchtown in a line with the cars of holiday-makers whose tents she could see pitched at the edges of nearby fields. The moonlight was such that without the aid of the interior lights she found an old pair of Wellies and a frayed anorak that she donned against the inevitable cold chill off the water.

But it was the evening gown, which was light, that proved an impediment, and pulling it up above her hips, she folded the silk material beneath the waistband of her underwear. Buttoned, the heavy coat covered her to mid-thigh, and she trudged on, noting the faint mauve flush to the east as morning approached.

There too was the ragged edge of a front, wispy and blue, like chalk, driving in with a speed that boded ill. It would storm in the new day, and Noreen hurried on. Until she reached the eminence of Carnsore Point, where the fields dropped down to the desert of dunes and the sea which was, she knew, about a mile distant.

It was there she came upon Daugherty's long, black Mercedes, glistening in the moonlight, and she waited what seemed like an age, debating how she would skirt it yet discover where Daugherty had gone—down into the dunes as he had the morn before? Why? The "bit of business" that he had been about with Athos? His allusion to greater wealth than all of Greenore Point could supply? With the approaching storm still very much to the east, it was windless there in the lee of the Point, but it would not be for long.

Finally the driver, in lighting a cigarette, settled her dilemma. He was slumped against one door, facing the moon, the storm and the sea to the east, his cap nearly covering his eyes. Noreen stole round behind him and down the steep incline to the dunes.

There with the cliff shielding her, she pulled the pocket torch from the anorak and played it over the sand, establishing, as her husband did in his investigations, a base line and then combing the area in progressive steps.

At length—how much time would she have before daylight would make her presence conspicuous to all for miles around?—she came upon a single footprint on the western slope of a dune. But whose it could be and how old, she had no idea. How had he gotten there, if not by car and foot? And for whom, then, could the car be waiting? Could it be his print from the day before, or was she, as she suspected, just chasing smoke and shadow? But she found another and then another, and—she believed—she had no choice but to follow their lead.

Amn't I the fool, she thought, out here in this God-forsaken place, traipsing after a callow egot of a man who could well be much worse, when I could be back in that bordello of a bedroom, sleeping soundly?

Then, the possibilities of what he could be about were endless—some other "bit of business," some small exchange contravening the customs laws, man to man, perhaps of something that would not be missed in the turmoil following the death of the owner of Greenore Eugenics.

But what could it be that would interest a man like Athos, who already had more of everything than he wanted? She remembered how uncomfortable he had seemed aboard his yacht and among his . . . things.

. Race horses were—she knew—his abiding passion. Thinking of the pedigree chart on the wall of Fionnuala Walton's office and what Daugherty had said to her of a line of "super horses," Noreen tightened the collar of the anorak against the breeze and hurried on.

The boots were a great improvement over the tennis shoes of the day before, except for one hole that let in more and more sand as she slogged on, following the single, occasional track. And it was when the prints veered toward the cliff face and the rocks that she found what she sought.

Having sat on a boulder and raised the hood of the coat so, she imagined, she looked just like a stone, all bent over to remove the shoe, she heard a man say, "No. For what I pay here, I buy more than just a horse. I buy a dynasty, like you said on the boat, but a *legitimate* dynasty with a knowable past. Without both sets of papers—the ones that prove he is who he is and then the others that prove he's not—hey, he's worthless.

"Years—ten, twenty, who knows—somebody's bound to write it up or question who was this nothing horse that sired all these champions. *How* and *why?* Then others they'll be jealous or mad they got beat. They'll want to find something. No—" There was a pause; Noreen had heard that voice before with its heavy and clipped accents. It was Nick B. Athos. "—I got my doubts."

"About *what*, Nicky?" said Daugherty. "You said it yourself—it's *him*, and I'm telling you it is. They syndicated him here for ten million. Had they circulated the shares in the States it would have been thirty. Isn't he the most beautiful animal you've ever seen?"

There was another pause in which Noreen thought she heard somebody laughing. "Look, Thomas—I got fields, whole rangelands of looks. Looks don't mean money. I hear you say that yourself, when you ride for me. And this is different. It's *business.* You know the difference? No salary, no . . . loyalty. Just the deal with the papers proving he's—"

There was another pause, and Daugherty said, "Taghmon."

"—or nothing. Now, would you take *my* word in a deal this big?"

"Certainly," Daugherty asserted.

"Then I shouldn't do business with you, my friend. You're a fool."

"But you said—"

"I said we had a deal—him *and* his papers. Now I say no papers, no deal. You don't like? Me neither."

"But—I've got no time. By noon tomorrow the courts 'll be in on it, solicitors, estate officers, the *police,* for Jesus' sake will be swarming all over the place. They'll find him missing, and somebody might look close and see who he *really* is. Or they'll find him missing, and you'll never get him out."

"No—*you*'ll never get him out. Me—I'll be gone. Without the papers it's no deal. How do I know what I'm buying? Your word? I want to see what Miss Walton done to make it all right and 'legal.' "

"*Know?*" Daugherty cried in a desperate tone. "You *know* what he looked like when he was racing. The stockings—it wouldn't do to cover them up, but the blaze on his face—? Here, you take him a moment. I brought along some bleach, thinking perhaps you'd pull this."

The light went out, and with a heavy clump that Noreen could feel right through the rock, some sort of door
closed.

Whipping her head around, she saw nothing but the
lightless cliff face, and she thought of all the tales she'd
heard of smugglers, who in the nineteenth century had
used the spits and dunes of southern Wexford to conceal
black market cargo and, later, guns and munitions.

But she also searched for a place to hide herself more
completely, yet still see in the direction of the light. And
she had only just crouched down behind a flat piece of
gray stone that some storm had thrust up, like a shelf,
when a heavy timbered door in a cut in the cliff face
opened, and she saw Athos holding the reins of an extraordinary horse while Daugherty dabbed with a cloth at the
animal's forehead.

Like the stallion she had viewed in the field near Greenore Eugenics, this horse was tall and classically propor-
tioned with long, sloping shoulders, a deep rib cage, short
cannons, and long forearms. But although this horse too
was a bay, its color was much lighter, Noreen saw as it
shied and moved into the light.

Daugherty was saying, "You can check its lip tattoo, if
you like. And its 'night eyes,' " by which he meant the two
usual means of identifying a registered horse, "though I
think you'll agree after seeing this that he is what I say."

Taking the reins from Athos, Daugherty turned the
animal away from Noreen and into the direct beam of the
overhead light in the cavern, which had been fitted out
as a kind of stable. "Now what do you say? Tell me you
haven't seen this horse before. Tell me it's not him."

Athos nodded, "Maybe. But them papers, they're everything. And tomorrow, not the next day or the next. I
go tomorrow. It's me who takes the chance—here and in

147

Australia, getting him off. And maybe he break a leg and then I got nothing.

"You? Tomorrow you buy this place, if you like." One of Athos's hands swept out; both men were still wearing evening clothes, and Noreen wondered where Athos's car was parked. Had Daugherty come with him or had the Mercedes returned to Wexford Harbor for both men? No —no time.

"Or get out, like you say. If not London or Paris, maybe someplace like Rio or Chile. I got some friends there you look up. Maybe then in a couple, three years you come see how my line is doing. I can arrange it, and a poor little country like this can't afford to tail one man specially on a chance he *might* have committed a crime.

"Buck up now, Tom. We still got a deal, if you got the papers."

And it was only then when Daugherty turned the animal around that Noreen realized what she was seeing.

The horse, far from having a small, scythe-shaped blaze on its forehead, now displayed a wide splotch of white that extended right down to its nose. Noreen knew that horse. Before it had been kidnapped and allegedly destroyed before a ransom could be paid she had watched, cheered for it, and won a fair amount of money on the animal on two occasions—the Derby and the Irish Sweeps —that would remain among her most vivid memories of what horse racing could be.

But as Noreen began to rise up from her shelter there in the rocks, the horse pricked its ears, then wheeled suddenly as though at the sound of an intruder.

It was then a palm clapped over Noreen's mouth, and she was lifted roughly from her concealment behind the shelf of rock and carried toward the two men.

"Oh, Christ!" said Daugherty. He had raised a hand to shield his eyes from the glare.

Athos asked, "Miss—?"

"Frenche," Daugherty supplied.

Athos's expression seemed suddenly despondent and almost sad. His eyes rose from her Wellies to her bare legs, the anorak, and finally her face. "Well—that's it." He turned to the horse and shook his head, then, glancing at Daugherty, moved past the man who still held Noreen off her feet, his hand nearly choking her. "You're worse than I thought, bringing her here. But it's something"—he shrugged—"you'll have to live with. First, no papers. Then this. I told you just me and you, so if it got out I'd know who to come for. Now? *Nothing.*"

"But, wait." Glaring daggers at Noreen, Daugherty stepped by her. "*I* didn't bring her here, Nicky. She's just a woman, for Jesus' sake. An old maid on the make on holiday. She must have followed my car here.

"Christ—let's not let her stand in the way of your getting yourself the stud of the century. You want the documentation? You'll have it in the morning or—feck it!—tonight. It's my brother and that bitch of his, is all, and I can deal with them. Or Machala. This one—?" Daugherty swung round, his dark eyes glazed, his lips tight and bloodless. "Just leave her now to me."

Athos's first laugh was short and sharp and mirthless, but the peal that followed conveyed a sense of cruel joy. "Like so far I've left everything else?" He shook his head. "Murder charges and me—we don't mix, and I give you 'til noon." He flicked his chin toward the door, and the man who held Noreen began to carry her away.

"But wait. What you do with her is more important to me than you. People'll place her with me, they'll know we were out together. Her family—"

"Just make sure you got the papers. Now I take the horse."

At the entrance to the cave were a half dozen of the crew from the *Amphitrite* still dressed in their white and sea-green uniforms but wearing heavy deck jackets and long-billed caps. Several carried snub-nosed automatic weapons and electric torches with brilliant, sealed beams.

Noreen heard the throbbing of the yacht's powerful engines before she actually saw it anchored lightless in a narrow channel about a mile from the cave. The banks were heaped with darker, compacted sand and muck, as though dredged in the recent past.

She was taken up the pneumatic lift, as was—she heard from a cabin—the horse some minutes later.

The vessel turned slowly then surged, it seemed to her, toward the sunrise and the sea.

"I demand to speak to Mr. Athos," she said to a steward who brought her a cup of dark Greek coffee and a bun. "I am not Noreen Frenche, as his accomplice, Daugherty, believes. I am Noreen McGarr, and my husband is Chief Superintendent of the Gárda Síochána, the police of this sovereign country.

"He knows I was out with Daugherty and aboard this yacht, and he'll have you stopped the moment I'm missed."

The man closed and locked the door.

10

Even from the hill above Greenore Eugenics, McGarr knew there was trouble at Binn na Rinn Farms. The night sky to the west was ablaze with an artificial light that muted through a spectrum from blue to gold. Above the farm the glow was punctuated by the navigation beacons atop the silos, which winked like six bloody stars. Below through the avenue of chestnut trees, McGarr could just make out the blinking, blue domes of several emergency vehicles.

Suddenly remembering his wife, he forgot his pain. Hurried on by the storm winds at his back, he rushed through field after field until he reached the road, where he ran.

In sheets the rain was driving off the sea. It beat on his neck and the back of his head and at first stung, then soothed, his tired eyes. In his mouth it tasted salty yet dry, like brine from a cup. It made him want more.

The Deux Chevaux was gone from under the chestnuts, but had been replaced, it seemed, by every type of vehicle, most with emergency beacons and police or media logos on their doors. Then a light in an arbor made the narrow doorway of the old farmhouse seem crowded with heads and shoulders, which were presided over by a stocky, blond man in a rumpled suit. McKeon, McGarr's desk sergeant.

His close-set, dark eyes brightened as they surveyed McGarr's bruised and puffy face. "Boys," he said to the journalists. "You can see the Chief's had his holiday bash. Pity the nose wasn't realigned, though it's the fond wish that's never fulfilled."

McGarr said nothing, though McKeon's attitude alone was reassuring. Certainly there would be no jest if anything had happened to his wife.

To the crowd, who now began barking questions at McGarr, McKeon said, "If yous can make some order amongst yous, yous'll be let into the mud room where Superintendent O'Shaughnessy will administer a silent benediction. If not—" A barrage of rain pelted the front of the farmhouse, and a complaint went up from the press.

"Chief! Chief McGarr!" some others shouted at his back. Bursts from strobe lights peppered the hall, into which O'Shaughnessy, McGarr's second-in-command, now stepped.

A tall, older man with pale, blue eyes and a sober manner, he did not acknowledge McGarr's cuts and bruises. Obviously having been called from an evening out, he was wearing a gray, brushed-linen suit with a lighter-colored handkerchief showing a precise three-eighth inch from the pocket. McGarr wondered if he had measured the margin. O'Shaughnessy opened a small black notebook.

"The call came in at quarter to one. From Stack. Said he himself had gotten a call from one of the victim's field hands who rooms above." A large thumb jerked to the ceiling. "Said things had not been right all night with what he calls blowing, and cars and people coming and

152

going. Said he'd heard a crash—glass breaking and then a thud, sometime before, but thought it was just the missus—the victim—in her cups, which was not unusual of a Friday night. But it was the light, about a half to three-quarters of an hour later that made him come down. That puts the time of death just about midnight."

O'Shaughnessy had led McGarr down the hall past men from the Technical Squad who were now waiting their turns to be let into the room in which, earlier, McGarr had seen Mna Daugherty in her rocker. Her bedroom, he now could see.

"He found her as she is. Strangled with the cord from the light. No prints. Nothing so far. The front door was left as always ajar, but, as you can see, the window is open as well."

"Has Noreen been about?" McGarr asked, before he stepped in.

O'Shaughnessy glanced up from his note pad. "Noreen, your—"

McGarr nodded.

"Should she have been?"

Knowing his staff would have checked every room and not wanting to explain what he now viewed as a mistake, McGarr only moved past O'Shaughnessy into the glare of Technical Squad lights. How far could he have strayed in a mere two-plus weeks that he had confused his marriage with his work, his holiday with the serious and sometimes dangerous business of life? Vigilance was necessary to maintain one's sense of self, and what was it somebody had said? "The judgment on a mistake in nature is death." From his own perspective it was not quite that severe, but he had had in his time several close calls, and almost all had been unexpected.

Then, how to justify the matter of his having allowed

Noreen to "step out," as it were, with a man McGarr now viewed as a suspect? It was something best left unrevealed, could he help it. Once more his hand strayed to the flask on his hip. The other palm had begun to throb again.

"Clean," said McAnulty, the Technical Squad Chief. "And quick." He shook his head. "As you can see, she reached out to grab at something to pull herself away, but there was only the lamp and the table with the phone and the glass."

Her corpse was slumped half out of the chair where she had struggled to free herself from the cord of the lamp. It had been slipped between two stout spindles of the rocker, around her neck, and then back between another two. There it had been pulled tight until—McGarr imagined—she expired. It was then made neat in a square knot that was now somewhat loose.

Her black dress was hiked up her thighs. One black pump had been kicked off. Her glasses were unbroken on a threadbare carpet by the side of the rocker, though the lamp and the glass had shattered when the table had been knocked over. The window was still open, as it had been when McGarr had viewed her earlier in the night.

A strobe sprayed the walls with light from—it seemed to McGarr—directly above his head.

"Will you get out of it," McKeon roared, collaring a photographer roughly and pulling him up the hall. "I told yous, the mud room. Now it's the yard."

"How'd they get here?" McGarr meant the press.

"They were phoned and not by us. All three papers and R.T.E." He meant *The Press, The Times,* and *The Independent* and Radio Telefis Eireann, which was the state-run radio and television network. "Directions and everything."

"Female voice?"

"No. Male."

McGarr glanced up and asked himself what he could say about the sight before him: some ugliness was at work on Greenore Point, some morbidity, a rot that had doubtless been festering for years to this result. In spite of the distortion of her grasping craftiness, Mna Daugherty had been a happy and by her own description a "jolly" woman whose hubris had been all too obvious in her attempt to make herself mistress of all she surveyed. But had she deserved to die?

McGarr again thought of his wife. "The moment Noreen gets here I want to know," he said, turning to the door. "Or this Tom Daugherty, the son."

"Is she expected?" O'Shaughnessy asked, but McGarr was supping from his flask.

In the sitting room he found six men still in pajamas or nightclothes. One wore only an undershirt and briefs, and his farmer's tan made him seem like he had dipped his head, neck, and forearms in a bucket of tannin.

Said Hughie Ward, another of McGarr's assistants, "Not much here but for this fella." He pointed to a large, obese man, who had been dozing on a Morris chair. "Jack Caulfield. Age fifty-seven, of Kilranell originally. Known familiarly as—" Ward glanced up, having decided not to continue with the description.

"Chow-Chow-Chow," said the man in his skivvies, as he poked at the coals of the fire. Far from humor, there was a kind of sadness in his voice. The others seemed similarly glum, and nobody laughed.

"Can you tell the chief what you told me, sir?" said Ward.

"It's what she called me," he said, "funning like she always was. A hard-headed woman, that's sure, and good with a pound. But, you know, if she hadn't a been, what would there've been for me and most of us—the dole or maybe worse." He had a tumbler of Wexford crystal in his hand. They had helped themselves to the decanter, which was nearly empty.

"But tonight, now," Ward prompted. "Tell the chief about tonight."

He paused dramatically, and in contrast to the hubbub coming to them seemingly from every other part of the house, the sitting room was filled only with the stillness of stares. The man basked in the attention.

His own eyes—large and cowlike in a rough, unshaven face—flickered up at McGarr. "Couldn't sleep. I'd been down to the pub with the boys. The bristlings I'd taken on the final pint were, with the wild and changeable weather and this storm, still leaping in me gut." He touched a hand to the protuberance of his stomach, which a yellowing undershirt made seem round and smooth. "Sensitive of late it's been."

Several of the men swapped glances, but nobody smiled.

"We left early, what with the hayin' we've to do in the morn, and it was maybe an hour or two later when I heard the Mercedes on the drive. Bein' most senior here, mine is the big room above the door, and I heard the woman get out. She thanked the driver—some sod from Wexford Town Tom hires for 'private' matters"—he winked—"and she stepped to the door.

"The car wheeled off, crunching the drive with its plump tires, like it does. But the woman—rosy and trim and quick, you know the type—didn't move from the doorway or I would have heard her step in the hall. I knew she'd gotten out alone, elsewise Tom, who's never without a word, would have said something. But instead of going along to her room, she waited until the car was a mere moan in the distance. Then she went back out across the yard and started up her Deux Chevaux, the one with the Dublin plates.

"A banger, it is. You'd know the sound anywhere. Two horses, it means in French, I'm told. Two cylinders, you see." He held up two fingers and said, *"Deux Chevaux."* He smiled shyly at McGarr. "We get a lot of foreigners here, now with the ferry."

Impatiently Ward tugged out a crease in the several sheets of statements he had taken. The man had obviously come to the point with which the young inspector was concerned.

"Then maybe a half hour went by. I played the radio to see if I could pull in somethin' in English, but on the short band, which is all I've got, I could only raise the Yanks and their propaganda and the Radio Moscow and theirs at the other end. I switched it off.

"It was then I heard another crunch on the drive and at first I thought it was the redhead returning. Car trouble, says I. Them Frogs—they make pretty things not worth a pig's trotter for wear.

"Then, you know, I was either finally dozin' or I didn't think to listen, but remembering back now—since I been told it's important—I can't seem to recall hearing the door open. It's got this little squeal, as the boys can attest, and maybe two, three minutes later I heard a hell of a crash, bang, boom, with glass breakin' from the back of the house and the missus's.

"Far be it from me to revile the dead, God rest her soul, but it's no secret she fancied the odd cup and would tope a bit on her own now and again. Many's the night us boys returned from the local to find her out on the dining room table or on the stairs or, once, right on the doorstep with the car—Tom's Mercedes—still ticking over out front. To make a long story short, I did not to my shame go down, though I would have wrung with these hands the neck of the villain what done it." In the quiet, Caulfield held up two calloused hands with thickly muscled wrists. He twisted his fists in opposite directions.

"Maybe a minute went by, not more, probably less and I heard that same step on the drive. Nature had called," his glance at McGarr was almost shy, "and I got up and in passing the window glanced out, though whoever it was was already up the drive under the trees. I listened hard, with my ear right on the open window in the toilet that catches every sound, it does, until I could only hear the blowing miles distant. Down by the Eugenics, I believe."

McGarr paused, considering what the man had said and what he knew of those he considered suspects in the first murder if not yet the second. At length, he asked, "How many years have you lived here?

"Ah—" His expression of helpful insouciance suddenly crumbled. "—since Mna and me were mere children. Cousins. Her husband, Dan, gave me this job of work when I was fresh from school. We came here together, her as"—his voice cracked—"mistress, and me as . . . whatever was needed, and I'll tell you true. I'm so torn up about this thing, that I can't for the life of me think of what I should do." He had bent his head, and a tear dotted the floor by his feet.

There were others who had looked away, and the man in his underwear, muttering something, opened the sideboard and pulled out a fresh bottle.

"Why is it you thought the . . . redhead had returned?" In the hallway, McGarr now heard McKeon say, "Tom Daugherty. Why, you're just the man we wanted to see."

A lower voice replied.

McKeon continued, "That'll be explained to you in a moment. Wait right here."

Said the fieldhand, "Light like, it was. Either a woman's step or somebody else who was trying to walk soft, but with all the shenannigans going on—the blowin' and all— I paid it no mind until I wondered at the missus's current bein' on and came down. She never suffered it to remain blazin' like that, and was always roaring at us to switch things off. I figured the whiskey had bested her again, and I'd help her to her chair.

"But—lo—there she was, choked blue like a calf in a loop and still warm to me touch, though the flame had been quenched from her entire. No pulse, no breath.

"I touched nothing, like they say, and phoned the police. Superintendent Stack."

Only the shoulders of Daugherty's tuxedo were spattered with rain, and lightly. Said McKeon, "Arrived here by staff car, he did. Driver and all. It's out in the yard. A Mercedes 300D, registered to T. A. Daugherty of this address. His nibs entirely and dressed to kill."

"Where's my wife?" McGarr asked.

"Your who? What's this all about?" Indignant, his eyes moved from man to man. He had slipped one hand stylishly into the side pocket of the tux.

"Noreen Frenche."

His eyes returned to McGarr, then glanced up the hall toward another group of men. "What do you think you're doing with my mother?" He moved forward, but McGarr stepped in front of him.

"Noreen Frenche—where is she?"

"Why, right where she should be, little man. Either in her bed but more likely mine."

Every head went back, and McGarr flushed with momentary anger that he quickly quelled, though he asked himself why the man—young and handsome, as he was, and connected with the horsing crowd that his wife so much admired—thought he could say that openly.

And for the first time in his married life he felt his footing on the brink of the chasm which was jealousy slip. Certainly she was young and attractive and, given his hours which were often interminable, she had had cause and opportunity to seek out some others' company. And then McGarr sometimes felt unworthy of her, though such insecurity came only when he was tired or drunk.

But any suspicion, based on the statement of what could easily be a murderer, was to say the least unfair, McGarr told himself. And he smiled. "It's a possibility we hadn't imagined, and we'll check it, we will. But what have you been doing since you dropped Noreen Frenche off here?"

The question plainly caught him by surprise. "A bit of business out on Carnsore Point, if you must know." Again he glanced down the hall. "You're not doing anything stupid, like arresting my mother for Fionnuala's—" Once more he attempted to move forward but McGarr stayed him.

"At midnight? What sort of business was that, and I'll tell you this—you can answer me here or in Dublin. It's all one to me."

Daugherty scanned the other faces. Furrows patterned his brow, and his head went down. "If it's Dublin, well then, it's Dublin, but I'll answer nothing without my solicitor present. I only hope for your sake you've not questioned my mother at this hour."

Bravado and a bluff and all the more pitiable considering the reality Daugherty would momentarily have to face. McGarr had half a mind to call him on it, though he remembered what the fieldhand had said about the lightness of the step on the drive. Then, Noreen would not have followed Daugherty for nothing.

"Where on Carnsore Point?"

"The very end."

"You were there for how long?"

"Until I returned here."

"Directly?"

Daugherty nodded.

"You have witnesses?"

"My driver."

Then Noreen might have chosen to wait awhile before returning or, because she or the Deux Chevaux had been seen, she might have decided to take herself off the case entirely. A third possibility was that she had chosen to follow whomever Daugherty had met with, if he was indeed telling the truth. McGarr sorely desired to know who that was and why at that hour of the night on which his mother was murdered.

And, given what McGarr himself knew concerning the whereabouts of the suspects in the first murder on the occasion of the second, he believed he had at least some purchase on the identity of the murderer, were there only one.

What now troubled him, however, were the last words that he had heard Mna Daugherty utter when he had looked in on her through the open window a few hours before. "Sure, I always said what's good for horses and cattle must have some application to family life. I'm only wanting a bit for me own. Tomorrow would be as good a time as any to patch things up." To whom? And could it somehow relate to the blowing, which Deirdre Walton and her son Dan believed she had had something to do with?

"May I go in to my mother now?"

Distracted, McGarr stepped aside and too late tried to reach for Daugherty's sleeve. Laboring under the delusion that his mother was still alive, Daugherty was in for a double shock—the fact of her death and the sight of her garroted there in the chair.

And indeed it was her very liveliness that made her death seem an impossibility. For all her unabashed homeliness and country cunning, she had been an engaging, colorful personality and one who, McGarr imagined, would be missed. Then, with her Daugherty could only have spent most of his life.

The men in the doorway made way for him, though he did not completely enter the room. Instead he remained in the hall, tilting his head first one way and then the other, almost in the way that she herself had when she had been alive. It was as though he were trying to see her at an angle that would deny the reality of the lamp wire tied in a post hitch, her open, depthless eyes and blue face, her tongue, which had lolled from a corner of her mouth and was a deep magenta color.

He then turned suddenly and blundered in one direction into some of the men and then the other way. McGarr had his flask out, which he offered him. "I think you have some idea who did this."

Daugherty stopped and seemed to consider the shiny tops of his patent-leather shoes.

When he said nothing, McGarr continued probing for a reaction. "No use trying to keep this one to yourselves. The press are amongst us now." McGarr waved the flask toward the hubbub, which was continuing in the mud room. "One of your acquaintances here on Greenore Point called them while you were about that bit of midnight business. Good job you got it done. Tomorrow it's the law and the courts and who knows what else—a new mistress or master there at the Eugenics."

McGarr only just ducked Daugherty's punch, which strayed wildly into the other men and sent the flask skittering across the worn deal floor, spewing its precious fluid.

"What's for him?" O'Shaughnessy demanded, after Daugherty had been restrained.

"Lesson in the ring," said McGarr, retrieving the nearly empty silver vessel and deciding he would fill it from a bottle in the sitting room sideboard. "Teach that at Port Laoise." Pronounced "Port-leash," the Midlands city was the site of an Irish prison. "I advise him to ponder that before morn.

"Where might I speak to you in private, Mr. Daugherty? Solicitor and all."

The man only swirled his shoulders and turned toward the door.

Ward glanced at McGarr, who nodded, meaning Daugherty should be followed. "But the chauffeur, he's to be grilled but good. Give him to Bernie." To O'Shaughnessy, he added, "I also want to know if it was also a man's voice that phoned the media and if, perchance, it stammered. Who was on the desk for us?"

"Rut'ie," O'Shaughnessy replied, referring to the Murder Squad's only woman.

McGarr nodded. She forgot nothing. "Then have her put a rush on the analysis of that chip of prismatic glass. And send somebody out to Carnsore Point to look around."

O'Shaughnessy glanced up from the pad on which he'd been noting the orders. "For what?"

"Oh . . . for any little thing that might turn up." McGarr

had in mind a Deux Chevaux and a redheaded woman; he wondered if, as she contended, he was addicted to alcohol and drank too much.

And instead of proceeding to the sitting room, he walked into the murdered woman's bedroom and used his handkerchief to lift her glasses from the floor. The lenses were soiled but intact. Bifocals for myopia with some mild correction above.

Could she have had two pairs? Not likely, considering how meager—*stingy* was more the word—she had been to herself. He glanced around the spartan appointments of the room and at her black dress and serviceable pumps. She hadn't *deserved* more or better, though she could afford it. McGarr rather thought so, from the little he knew of her. It was a side effect (hangover?) of the doctrine of guilt *because* of one's birth, which he had never been able to understand. Wasn't the fact of life a matter for joy? He decided he would fill the flask, addiction or no.

Back out in the hallway, he said, "In the morning I want every eye doctor and optician in the area canvassed for prescriptions for this list of suspects." Reaching toward O'Shaughnessy, McGarr was handed the much taller policeman's notebook, in which he wrote the names of the surviving members of the Daugherty and Walton families.

11

Greenore House was locked tight, and McGarr had to walk round to knock at the back door. There the newly risen sun was frazzling the wet grass, making it too brilliant to look at directly, and he turned his gaze to the house. Through tall kitchen windows he could see Siobhan, the older sister, moving about. He could hear water running and sounds of her working at a sink.

He rapped on the rippled glass door, then knocked, and finally struck its wooden margin with the heel of his fist. Yet she did not look up. He then stepped out onto the lawn there into what he believed was her line of sight and waved his arms. "Miss Walton!" he hollered. "Miss Walton!"

Finally, frustrated and needing to get in if only for a cup of something hot and to be near a phone, he tossed a pebble at the kitchen windows and then another, and at last she glanced up and seemed not to see him at first. It took her some time to get to the door.

Through the rippling, as though through water, he watched those large, pink hands dry themselves on an apron and then search for the key, which was played in the lock for a while before the door relented.

"So—it's you again," she said without moving from the doorway. "Any luck?"

McGarr did not understand.

"With the blowers." Her eyes, the corner of one of which was now so raw it looked bloody, did not assay his cuts and bruises. Instead, they seemed to be focused up over his head, and he wondered how much sight she actually had.

"Well—you'd best come in, if that's what you want." She turned and moved into the house, her step made ponderous by her heavy, swollen legs. "And mind the door. We're damp enough here without letting in the dew."

In midsummer, McGarr thought? Most Irish houses were then opened to any drying breeze, and he noted her appearance. Today again she was wearing some worn housedress with a heavy cardigan buttoned high on her chest. McGarr guessed she was in poor health, as she paused on the landing before tugging herself up the three final stairs.

In the kitchen, he waited to see if, like most other Irish women he knew, she would offer him a cup of tea as a matter of form. When she only turned and regarded him with her bloodshot gaze, he moved past her to the stove where on a trivet he saw a coffee pot. It was empty, and in trying to twist it open, McGarr burnt his good hand.

Swearing and dropping it to the range top, he reached for a pot holder but even pressing the pot into his body could not twist the top off. The injured hand was now weak and it throbbed.

"Allow me," said Siobhan, reaching past him with her bare hands. Snatching up the steamer, she raised it to her chest and, swirling her large shoulders, turned it loose.

With deliberation she then unscrewed the pieces, setting them down on a metal table. "Could it be you're too well bred to have asked? Black beans or brown? Black, I'll wager. Strong and straight. A man's man."

Did McGarr detect a note of sarcasm in her tone? He believed he did. "Like Dan," he said. And Dan Jr., he thought.

"No—he drank tea, when he had to, and it was Fionnuala who bore the real strength. Didn't she outlive him?" Siobhan had to bend her head to read the labels on the coffee tins.

"But she was murdered."

The large woman looked up. "So, God love her, she was."

"By Mna Daugherty," McGarr prompted. When she said nothing, he added, "Who's been murdered herself."

Her head turned to him. The goiter on the side of her face seemed as if it were pulsing, though her eyes were steady.

"Not surprised?" he asked.

"Nor bereaved," she answered, turning back to the coffee pot.

"Any idea who did it?"

"None."

"Any concern that it might have been the same person who murdered your sister?"

"Why should that concern me?"

"Who knows?—you could be next."

"Not likely—I who have led a good life, injuring nobody, incensing none."

"And who did your sister injure?"

"Well"—she leaned closer to the tins and squinted— "there might have been some who so thought."

"Like Mna Daugherty?"

"I said that yesterday, and I'll say it now with no disrespect for that woman's memory."

"Or your niece."

She turned the splotched eye to him. "Like what, pray? Mna could not have wanted better for her last son, afflicted as he is."

"But for herself?"

"Think you her an unlikely mother? If so, you're not much of a judge. Like any woman worthy of her sex, she lived through her children, once born."

"Lose your glasses?"

"What glasses?"

"Your eyeglasses? You've a broken blood vessel in the corner of your left eye, I'm sure you've noticed. Dangerous that. It can lead to complications."

"And you—your face looks like a round of ash after an ugly chukker. No, sir"—she selected the proper tin and straightened up—"I wear no glasses, now or ever. The eye is a muscle," she made a fist, "which must be exercised. Loss of sleep is the cause of this." She pointed to the eye, while she regarded McGarr who was just her height. "And with a night or two of rest it'll clear, so it will.

"Hot milk?"

McGarr shook his head. What his coffee required he had in his flask, and he had nearly left the kitchen when he remembered one other matter.

"Deirdre's mother," he said from the door to the hall. "Her name was—?"

"Dympna." Siobhan was back at the sink, washing the coffee pot. The kitchen was otherwise spotless.

"When did she die?"

She shook her head. "I don't know. Haven't I put it out of my mind? Sometime in the Sixties. Eight or nine."

"When Deirdre was what age?"

"Sure—I couldn't tell you, but young."

"She died of—?"

"Consumption. The damp, like I told you of at the door." She had completed washing the pot and now rejected two dish towels before selecting a third to dry it.

"And who raised Deirdre?"

"Who do you think, and her with family."

McGarr considered what he knew of Fionnuala's life and the fact that Machala too had been employed at Greenore Eugenics. "By you then?"

"At least one of us had to show her right from wrong."

On the stairs up to the second floor McGarr met Machala, the other surviving sister, who rather surprised him, her step on the carpet soundless as she descended. He tried to catch a few drops of coffee that splashed from his cup, and a hot splotch landed in the palm of his injured hand. "Damn," he muttered.

"Problems, Inspector?" she asked, her black dress too tight, the side slit too daring for mourning. The rake of the padded shoulders of her jacket was too extreme, the effect of her black pillbox cap with face net too histrionic. It made her face seem chalky and cadaverous, her light blue eyes unreal. They flashed over his face. "I can see you have. Don't ask for my help. I'm off to see the wizard."

McGarr was unsure what she meant. He knew that the Waltons were expected at court in—he glanced at his watch; 9:10—fewer than two hours. "Will he grant you or your daughter his wish?" he chanced.

She moved right past him. "*My* daughter. Thank the good Lord I have none of that. Pests, children. Demanding, covetous, and ungrateful."

"You must be thinking of Deirdre," he said.

"As were you with your allusion. No, Deirdre has

proved herself the *ideal* child, but, alas, she's not mine."

Her change of mood from the day before rather surprised McGarr. "How so, *ideal?*" He could not help but admire the shape of her ankle, the spare, clean lines of her back. With the exception of Siobhan, whose proportions were large, the Waltons, like the Daughertys, were a handsome family. He did not wonder at their desire to mate. Had the woman before him been so moved?

"Precocious, I'd say," she said now from the front hall. "And you'll get no more from me. Unless, of course, you're free tonight." Her laugh carried the ragged edge of hysteria, which was clipped abruptly by the closing of the heavy front door.

On the second floor, McGarr moved down the carpeted hall until he reached the niece's bedroom. Without knocking, he tried the door. The bed did not appear to have been slept in and all remained as he had seen it on the day before—the pictures of horses, the tack hanging from clotheshorses and the like, the smell of saddle soap, dubbin, and the stables rather strong.

And in the new daylight, the coppery lights of the attic were wan and pink, and McGarr, easing the door to, looked at the array of farrier's tools hanging from the pegs behind the door. How tall, he wondered, would one have to be to wipe the dust from that wall up to six or so inches above the top row of pegs.

About—he reached up—his own height, which was five eight or a bit taller and provided a chair or a trunk had not been available. He looked in back of him—not a trunk. They were too heavy. A chair? It would have had to have been gotten from downstairs, he surmised, and would the murderer have chanced that?

Setting the coffee cup on the floor, McGarr hunkered

down before the trunk in which he remembered having seen the Walton family Bible with the raised leather letters. It was there, half under several journals, though—like the floors, the walls and the farrier's claw—it had been wiped clean of dust.

Propping the heavy volume on his knees, McGarr eased open the cover to find that the seventeenth-century Bible had been brought with one Harrold Cranshaw Walton when he had been awarded ". . . all the rebel lande from Greeneoar to Kern Soare Points including all rights and perquisites, for his service to Parliament and country during the late insurrection in Irelande." One of "Cromwell's bastards," as those who had taken part in the vicious, punitive expedition in Ireland and had then been rewarded with expropriated land were known to the Irish, in some cases right down to this day.

There followed lists of births, deaths, and marriages, one to a Cecilia (Sheilah) Daochartie whose first son by Alexander Crittenden Meeres Walton inherited the family estate. That in 1787.

The last page, which he supposed included the births of the last two children of William Bedeman Cranshaw Walton and Jane Wiley Wilson Walton—Dympna and Fionnuala and the former's issue, Deirdre, whose past now interested him most—had been removed. *Not* torn from the hand-stitched and (was it?) parchment volume, but rather carefully cut using something like a straightedge and a razor. Such a removal had taken time, and why? More than ever McGarr believed he had an idea.

And how old could she be, he wondered? Twenty. Twenty-one or -two? Younger? Certainly her skin, clear and downed with the fine blond hairs that he had noticed the day before, made her no older.

Leaving the chair he advanced on the other trunks, and

searching through the journals that Fionnuala Walton had compiled assiduously since she was twelve years old, he discovered a gap. The volume for the year 1966 was missing. Turning back to the first trunk, he again rummaged through its contents but found no journal for that year.

Yet from 1 January to, it seemed, 31 December and nearly in the entry for every other day of the following year was some reference to Deirdre, then so much a baby that she required a wet nurse. The note for 17 February caught McGarr's eye.

"Little could we have known, when apprised of what Siobhan and Machala first thought of as the 'problem' of Deirdre's coming, the joy and life that she could bring to this house. I swear that Siobhan is a new woman, and Machala, far from staying out half the night and never being seen on weekends, is now her constant companion. Opening the front door when I return from work, I inevitably now hear singing or laughing or at any rate the sounds of voices and not that deathly silence which has possessed this house for far too long. It is, as Dan himself has told me over and over again, life itself that matters, and he was as ever right in exhorting me to proceed with this course."

After more minutes spent in perusing some earlier journals and finding no mention of either Deirdre or Dympna, McGarr checked his watch—9:43—and moved back to the trunk, which had been found open on the day of the murder. He had little time, wanting to get to Wexford Town before the 11:00 o'clock meeting of the court on the matter of the Walton will. Having been requested by the now also murdered Mna Daugherty, the petition would not now be denied. Its contents might well prove central to any solution of two murders.

McGarr glanced down at the wedding portrait of the

handsome couple whose marriage was never in the usual way consummated. "6th June, 1947," the caption read, and he pieced through the trunk until he found the journal for the appropriate year.

Knowing he had at most ten minutes, McGarr began scanning its entries quickly, letting his eyes run down the middle page if only to corroborate what Siobhan had told him of those days. And far from merely having related the events of those times, it was as if she had appropriated her sister's thoughts.

". . . the wailing, the crying from the hedges, the hills, as though from some poor, dying, defenseless thing," he read. Then, "desperate and pitiable in its sound." Hadn't those been Siobhan's words exactly? A coincidence, he asked himself? A certain phrasing that the sisters, given their shared background and long tenure together, shared?

It was then that Siobhan, like a soundless wraith whom he had summoned, appeared in the doorway of the attic, her eyes riveted on the journal in his hands. "You've a phone call."

"Who is it?"

"Far be it from me to ask."

McGarr kept the journal in his hands as he stepped by her to descend to the landing and the phone on the stand in the hall below.

"Are you taking that away?"

"I might. Why?"

"Because it's ours. Our sister's. And we're to have it back."

It was O'Shaughnessy on the phone.

"The oil on the rag is dubbin. Special order. At one time Callaghan's of Dame Street supplied it by volume, but—"

McGarr completed the thought. That firm had gone

out of the tack and equipage business several years before and now was merely a sports clothier in the Brown Thomas department store on Grafton Street.

"It's available in Britain, of course," O'Shaughnessy went on, "but Callaghan's records, which still exist, say that Greenore Eugenics bought a large supply about ten years ago—all that Callaghan's had left, to be exact. Auction.

"As to the voice that phoned in the Daugherty murder. Rut'ie says it was male, young, and had a pronounced stammer. The same for the papers, each and every one of them.

"No word on the eyeglasses yet. Too early.

"Then there's the matter of Noreen's Deux Chevaux. It was found"—he paused—"near Carnsore Point. Stack went up there himself with every man he could muster, but . . . nothing. The storm wiped out every print. Even tire tracks had been all but expunged. She's not returned to the Daugherty place nor to Greenore Eugenics. I've placed men there as well.

"The Navy. I've taken the liberty of alerting them. And the Coast Guard. Customs. The ferry."

For a body, McGarr thought, suddenly feeling very bleak. He turned around to glance down the hall toward the light through the tall window on the stairway and found Siobhan standing not far distant, regarding him.

"Get a hold of Tom Daugherty," said McGarr. "Grill him. That chauffeur."

"Him we've got, as you ordered. But nothing, Bernie's convinced. He said he put down his hat and went to sleep, and it seems that's the truth of it. Says he, he dropped Noreen off at Binn na Rinn Farms, then proceeded out to the Point where, according to what Daugherty had told him, he just waited. Maybe about a half hour before we saw him at the farm, Daugherty merely arrived there and asked to be taken home. How he got there, where he'd been—?

"Hughie was in touch last at half nine, when Daugherty —who spent the night rummaging through the office at the Eugenics—tried to start an old Austin registered to the victim. The first one. Fionnuala—"

"Walton," McGarr supplied, eyes on the old woman.

"Not long after, another old car pulled in. An antique Jag, an XK 140 registered to Machala Walton. A middle-aged woman got out, dressed in—"

"Black," McGarr said.

"—and not long after that she and Daugherty left together, Hughie picking them up after they'd passed beyond his observation point. But with only beaches and fields—"

McGarr knew what he meant. It would be difficult to tail anybody in such open country, much less a local driver in a quick, agile car. "Well, they're probably off to discover their fortune, anyway."

"At court in Wexford Town."

"The same. Look—I'll be there myself, but nobody's to leave that building after the proceeding. Teams. If you need men, order them. I'll be there myself, but I want Bernie—"

There was a crash in the hall below, as the heavy door burst open and smacked into its jamb. "Siobhan! Siobhan!" shouted a voice that McGarr recognized as Deirdre's. "It's Tom, he's got a gun and he's taken Machala—" They then heard somebody scaling the stairs rapidly, two at a time. When arriving at the second floor, the niece looked up and stopped suddenly.

"Oh—it's you," she said to McGarr. "That's just as well." She turned to Siobhan. "All this killing must stop. Dan's

beside himself over his mother. After"—she blinked—
"the stables last night, he went back to the farmhouse to
tell her that we'd relent and sell her the land. Anything
to let the marriage go through and end all the violence."

McGarr was listening closely. Somehow he remembered that it was young Daugherty himself who had insisted on the violence on the night before.

"He *found* her there!" she cried, tears bursting from
her eyes. "Now he won't get out of bed. He says Tom can
have the blasted horse and the papers for all he cares. And
you and Machala the estate. He even says it's off between
us, so you've got your wish."

"*My* wish?" the old woman began to say, but Deirdre
cut her off.

"It's time for the police, no matter the loss, and—"

"Which horse?" McGarr asked. "What papers?" It was
what would have interested his wife.

"Ah—" She swirled her head, the ponytail whipping
against her shoulders, her blue eyes suddenly bright with
anger, "—the 'experiment.' Fi's and Dan's—my Dan's father." She glanced up at him. "You don't know yet?"

Said Siobhan, "And leave it to you to tell him."

"What? Think you it's of no moment here?" the girl
demanded. "We're speaking of Machala who is now your
only sister. And if we don't or won't or can't bring ourselves to say something, we're worse than Tom who at
least now has declared his intentions."

"The *experiment?*" McGarr asked in a small voice.

The niece turned to him. "To create a thoroughbred
sire line that would produce champion after champion,
with the get breeding true time after time.

"It was," she wagged her head and, after glancing at
Siobhan, looked away, "a kind of long shot, I guess. Something they began about two score years ago, more as

176

something to do to keep them together—she told me—after things between them had begun falling apart."

McGarr tried to recall the little he had chosen to know about horse breeding. "But wouldn't that require champion stock?"

The girl's eyes moved off toward the window. "Not necessarily. World-famous breeders have built their reputations on breeding champions from indifferent stock. In this case, however"—with a look that McGarr judged was defiant, she fixed her aunt's gaze—"it was the best, the *very* best."

"And Greenore Eugenics breeds the very best?" If so, why had McGarr not heard of the stud before having been summoned here.

"But of course. *None* better," she went on archly.

Said Siobhan, "Well, I've to dress for the solicitor in town. I should advise you to do the same."

"Do you know that Tom has a gun? He held it to Machala's temple to get her to go with him."

"Like his father before him. A mucker. Would that he shoots himself, and it's not a horse or papers or that foolery with eugenics that's been going on around here for forty-plus years that's 'of moment,' as you say, but the Walton family name and Greenore House and its holdings.

"Tom? He'll not harm Machala, and I hope she knows that. He wouldn't dare." Siobhan turned and trudged down the hall toward her bedroom.

"And they did it? Fionnuala and Dan?" McGarr prompted the young woman, tightening his ear to the phone to make sure O'Shaughnessy was still there.

The girl plunged her hands in her jodhpur pockets and raised her shoulders. "To Fi's very great surprise. Are you planning to do something about this?" she asked.

McGarr pointed to the phone and nodded. "If I can understand what it's about."

She sighed and looked away. "Well—Dan, the father, was very observant and knowledgeable about horses. In that way too they made a . . . natural pair, but for too many years here they merely messed about with less than premier animals and got only acceptable results. You know, many wins but no great victories, and the truth was that they carried on only because they had the cushion of Fi's money.

"The day came though when Dan became ill, and they knew it was terminal. It was then that Fi, who had until then been rather cautious with her money, decided she would buy and breed for the best. Her immediate aim"—the green eyes strayed from McGarr's—"was to produce one real champion before Dan died, but it was not to be." A tear broke from the corner of one eye and tracked down her cheek.

"Peter?" O'Shaughnessy asked through the phone, though McGarr said nothing. It was, he believed, the dimension of the case that until now he'd been missing.

"And the horse in question, the one that's missing, is the result of that program?"

"Not the result, the horse upon which she had placed those hopes." The niece then sobbed and turned away toward the window that looked to the west and Binn na Rinn Farms.

"But just the *one* horse?" McGarr asked.

"Sure, we have good mares—some of the best in Ireland —and foals and now some two-year-olds, but the sire, which would be necessary to establish and sustain a line —" She turned to McGarr. "On the night of the afternoon on which my aunt was murdered, Tom Daugherty and nobody else secreted the stallion away from our stables and we've not seen it since.

"Dan, my Dan, went straight to the stables, the moment I told him about my having found Fi. But it was gone, even then. The papers? They were in the Eugenics' safe, we think, and Machala," she lowered her voice, "acting for herself and Siobhan, I believe, got those when there would have been more than enough to go round were the three parts—the sire, the mares, and the documentation—kept together. But Tom wanted it all, and since he has the most valuable and salable part—well, now you know."

McGarr was not certain he did, and yet again he thought of his wife, wishing she were with him. "Have I heard of this horse?"

"Sure—if you were in horses you would have." She folded her arms, and McGarr stepped around her to read her face.

"What's the name?"

"Taghmon," she said in a small voice.

McGarr searched his memory but was positive he had never heard mention of such an animal, and he so often in the company of horsing people. Then again, he had made it a point not to listen.

"But the mother now," he pressed. "Where did she fit in? Could he have taken it to her farm?"

The girl seemed to smirk. "He didn't dare, not wanting to cast suspicion upon himself or the mother, who, I'm sure, knew of it but must only have been interested in whatever advantage she might wrest in taking possession of our land. It was her sole concern. She didn't care damn-all about horses.

"And he could have taken it no place else that would be

in any way public, given the potential value of the animal and the fact of the murder. Don't think we haven't thought of where or searched, but the vicinity is much more Tom's place than mine or Dan's. We've spent too much time away. Or the mother's. Like Siobhan," again her voice went low, "I don't think she traveled farther than Wexford Town. The gossip has it that from the day she set foot in Binn na Rinn Farms, Mna Daugherty did not sleep one night away from that house."

"Is this horse why no word, no news of your aunt's death leaked out?"

The flash of her eyes seemed contemptuous to McGarr, and he thought of his first meeting with her. "Of course. It was the biggest thing to happen here in a century. When raced, the foals of those dams will make history. Already their performance on our gallops is phenomenal. Managed properly, brought along slowly with careful breeding and strict, monopolistic control, that sire represents"—she looked off—"the sort of fortune that could last a family for . . . generations."

"Taghmon," McGarr said mostly to himself, again trying and failing to place the animal. "A *premier* animal?"

She looked away. "A horse that had been ignored but Fi with her background in genetics knew could be combined with the proper mares to produce remarkable results, *if* brought along incrementally. In that way we could show the racing world that we possessed not one super horse but an entire line."

She then turned to McGarr, as though challenging him. "Would *you,* then, have spoken of it, not knowing for sure who would inherit the estate and knowing that any word might cause Tom, out of fear of what the police might conclude, to destroy the animal or sell it quick to get it out of the country? The possession of any part of such a venture alone is valuable, and there was the chance that somehow we might have retrieved the stallion ourselves.

"Then, having the records of how Fi and Dan had gone about it, my Dan and I thought perhaps there was a chance we might do the same. It would take time, certainly, but we've plenty of that," she added with an innocence which for the first time revealed her youth and which McGarr considered rather charming. "Then," she added, "a breeder's word is her bond. As Mna Daugherty pointed out to Dan, when he went to her to find out if she had the horse or if she knew where Tom was keeping it, any murder, especially of the founder, could prove a disaster from which we might never recover."

"When was that?" Something did not ring true in what she was saying, but McGarr could not guess what.

"The morning after Fi's murder. Breakfast."

When Noreen was there, thought McGarr. "Then who murdered your aunt?"

"Tom," she said without hesitation. "He'd been after her to let him begin running Tomhaggard Joe, which is what the most promising of the two-year-olds is called. He wanted to take him to any and every race they could enter. If he won by the margins they expected, they could run one of the other young ones and then another and slowly, like that, they could have brought them on."

"And she?"

The niece looked off at the scene presented out the window there at the second-story landing. "Fi decided to wait another generation. She said that any success would only pressure them to enter bigger races and that the 'experiment,' as she termed it, wasn't ready yet."

McGarr cocked his head. At his father-in-law's stud, every win—even a dash of a Sunday afternoon—was welcome, and he could remember having heard over and over again that only through competition of the highest order could any promising horse prove itself.

"Then who murdered Mna Daugherty?" McGarr had the telephone receiver in his good hand; his concern for his wife was now very high and centered, it seemed, in the palm of his aching hand.

She cocked her head. Tears had filled her eyes, and in blinking one fell to the floor. "Tom?" she asked in a small voice that rose in question.

"Then it was Dan who phoned the police in Dublin?"

"Yes, the moment he got back to the stable. 'This time, we'll tell the world!' he roared. 'No covetous secrets. No obfuscations in the service of greed.' He was like . . . like a madman."

"And how would he have gotten to the farm? By the road?"

"I should imagine so. It was night and that storm was nearly upon us, though there's a more direct route through the fields to the back door."

"Without walking on the gravel?"

She nodded.

"Dympna was your mother?"

Another nod.

"She's dead?"

Yet again.

"When did she die?"

"When I was born, I've been told."

"And where was that?"

"Leeds."

McGarr thought for a moment: in young Daugherty's condition, walking would have been painful and in spite of the storm approaching from the east there had been a bright moon in the western sky.

Into the phone, McGarr said, "Liam?"

"Yes, Peter."

"Catch that?"

"Most of it. The niece, I assume?"

"Listen now—I want a priority rush on birth and death dates for both families. Central records. Right away. In particular I want the date of the death of one Dympna Walton, who might be listed at this address but more likely someplace in Britain. I want all her essentials— marriage, children, the like. Try Leeds, of course."

The niece turned and moved slowly toward the door to her room.

Then, what had Noreen said when Mna Daugherty and he had run into her in the hall outside the sitting room at Binn Na Rinn Farms? ". . . dinner and a bash on a yacht."

"And on that request to the Navy—Noreen went to some party aboard a yacht last night, someplace close enough to Greenore Point that she was able to get back by midnight. Rosslare, probably. Or Wexford Town. Let's see if we can find out which boat and who owns it and proceed from there."

After ringing off, he remembered something else—how Siobhan had told him that Tom had been with her in the kitchen on or about the time of Fionnuala's murder. If, as the niece contended, he had proceeded directly to the stables and taken the stallion, then he had to have known of that woman's death.

He remembered the door on the long hallway of bed-rooms that Siobhan had returned to on the night of her sister's murder. Without knocking, he opened the door.

Siobhan was standing near a closet, bending over to fit on a pair of shoes. She was wearing a black dress, and on the bed was the long-barreled shotgun she had used on the night before.

"You said that on the afternoon of your sister's murder

Tom Daugherty did not go up to see her. Instead he left your kitchen and returned to his work at Greenore Eugenics. You said you watched him yourself from the window over your sink. That window looks northeast, not south. Then, your sight, like your hearing, is poor. You scarcely saw me at twenty feet. You lied. Tom Daugherty did go up to her. He knew she was dead, which was why he went directly for that stallion."

She glanced down at the gun. "If anybody could have run this place after Fionnuala, it was Tom. It seems now, though, that he wants more. Yes"—she turned the raw eye on McGarr—"I lied. Deirdre and Dan—they'll only make a muck of things." She raised a wrist to hold her watch close to her face. "And soon."

Knocking on the niece's door, he heard a weak, "Come in," and found her lying facedown on the bed.

"I'm sorry to disturb you once more, but I wonder—would you have a supply of dubbin about. It's only my own curiosity I'm satisfying," he went on in a conversational manner. "Pardon my saying so, but it's the odor in here. The tack and all—"

Pointing to the closet, she said, "In the trunk there. I try to keep the door closed and the heat away from those things."

"But you found it open the night of the afternoon of your aunt's murder."

"It was the first thing I noticed. The smell was stiff."

There in the trunk McGarr discovered a large, silver tin of dubbin, "Callaghan's, Dame Street, Dublin" stenciled in ornate gold letters on the side. Opening the tin he found a rag from which clots of dust were still clinging. The dubbin was nearly gone.

"You'll soon be needing more," he said as he was leaving the room.

"Sure, we've plenty down at the stables."

He stopped at the door. Without turning back to her he asked as though it were of no moment, "Your Aunt Siobhan—what happened to her eyeglasses?"

"How would I know?"

"She should take to wearing them more often. Eye strain. I reckon she's broken a blood vessel in one."

There was a pause, and then in a weary voice the girl answered, "She says she doesn't need them, though her vision in dim light is poor. She puts them down then complains that they're lost. They'll turn up, bye and bye. They always do."

McGarr did not think so.

12

Ward found the Jaguar on the dock near the ferry, shuddering, one door open, the engine still ticking over. But neither Daugherty nor the woman was in it. Where could they be, he wondered, scanning the harbor.

On the ferry, which had been docking when he had raced down the hill? Now it had begun to off-load its fares: tandem lorries that clanked over the dock plates and piped clouds of diesel smoke as they geared up the hills, tails of tiny, timid cars in their wake; crowds of luggage-toting Continentals with bikes, knapsacks, and plastic sacks of duty-free, who were streaming toward buses and the train for their holidays. No. Why? It would not depart for at least an hour.

Then, Daugherty had driven with the abandon of a man with a purpose. As Ward had watched him from afar through binoculars, he had stuffed the woman into the front seat and had hurtled through the breeding facility. Ward had scarcely reached his car before the Jaguar had disappeared from sight, and his finding it there was more intuition—where else was there to go in the area?—than skill. Conclusion? Daugherty knew where he was heading and it could not be to the ferry, which was a trap.

Ward switched off the engine and closed the door, then radioed his position to the Rosslare Gárda barracks, hating to admit that, like some novice fresh off a beat, he had lost his man.

And here of all places, he thought—country so open you could see for miles with only this harbor for cover. Not the Dublin he was used to with its webs of narrow streets and laneways winding back on each other. A flock of seagulls burst from the far end of the pier as some engine or other blatted to a start.

In Dublin he, like every other experienced cop he knew, *had* lost a man, but not many, and it was understandable there. But *here?* He shook his head and turned to the east and the great, bloody sea which under a fair and nearly cloudless summer sky was still roiling after the storm of the night.

It was then that it hit him—the high, whining howl of some boat which, because of the pier, he could not see. As though stung, he leapt forward and began running, dodging gangs of dockmen. He sprinted past handcarts, dollies, and forklifts until at length, it seemed, he gained an open space where he saw Daugherty at the end of the pier, slipping a line free from a bollard.

Ward shouted. He screamed, but the wind off the sea buffeted back his words, and Daugherty, spinning around, raised his arm. Ward went down, the report of the gun sounding no louder than the snap of a twig. When he raised his head, Daugherty was gone, and he reached the dock as the launch—some long, snipe-nosed sports craft, all forward deck with little cockpit—canted skyward and roared away from the pier. Daugherty's backward glance was cursory.

A man with something on his mind, thought Ward. And

well he should. The boat was obviously not large enough to cross the Irish Sea, and they'd find it and him soon.

"He had a gun," somebody hollered so close to Ward's ear that he jumped. It was a dockman with several others behind him. "And who knows, these days, why? But the woman"—the man shook his head—"she was scared skinny, she was."

And well she should be, thought Ward. He wondered about the Chief's wife, and if she'd been heard from since.

She hadn't. And from where she sat the wall of glass before her looked like the antiglare screen on a VDT. It polarized the light and made the scene of a wild and storm-tossed sea seem flat and patterned, like pastel colors glimpsed through a wire mesh.

As such, it was an effect that both attracted and repelled her. She thought of its artificiality as the most conspicuous of the many Veblenesque excrescences with which the boat was laden. But at the same time she found the tumbling seascape with its ragged white thunderheads to the west appealing in the extreme. Like the cinema to which she was addicted, it was a panorama that, she imagined, cost a fortune and she could view for hours on end.

It seemed like that too. Twice now she had refused drinks of coffee, tea, or the Campari and soda that Athos once in a while touched his lips to and set aside with a sour expression, watching the glass as though he considered drinking it some sort of self-imposed penance. He was sitting beside her on the bridge of his yacht, having come to the cabin in which she'd first been placed to explain that a terrible but necessary mistake had been made, given Daugherty's presence.

"Him? He's over his head. Trying to get rich too fast. If money came so easy, you'd see one country filled with billionaires—Greece." The attempt at humor seemed so strange coming from him that Noreen felt obliged to smile.

"And don't worry," he had gone on, "I don't come by this"—he had gestured to mean the yacht—"by hurting people. Most times. Specially none whose husband is the police."

And when Noreen had raised an eyebrow, he had added in a serious tone, "This thing between him and me—" Athos had paused, as though reconsidering it. He then shrugged. "I want it, that's all. My way. You'll see."

Handing her a pair of binoculars, he now said, "You look at that and tell me what you see?" He pointed to a speck that had just appeared on the horizon and, she imagined, without the special windscreen would not have been visible. Moving at speed, it soon became the prow of a small boat with two figures visible in the cockpit. More than a few seconds later, she recognized the flowing silver hair, the dark, tanned features and black tie of the one behind the wheel. The woman beside him Noreen had never before seen.

"The man is Tom Daugherty. The woman I don't know."

"*Man?* You think?" said Athos, accepting the glasses which she handed back. "Me—I check him out, like I check out everybody. And I see a boy who never really left home and his mother. Maybe never will."

As the boat neared the yacht, Athos turned to his captain. "Bring them here."

To Noreen, he added, "The fewer to watch, the better. I let you for the education." Again he tried to smile, but he looked out toward the sea suddenly, as if remembering something.

The wind staggered Daugherty as he stepped up onto

the bridge, and the woman required the arm of a crewman.

Daugherty paused, as a hatch was opened for him, and he studied Noreen and Athos, then Noreen again. She was now wearing yachting whites with the *Amphitrite* logo on the pocket.

Two other crewmen now appeared behind the woman. One held an Uzi machine gun, its stubby barrel pointed toward the floor. From behind her port side, Noreen now heard a latch disengage and felt a sudden shock in her ears, as though the pressure there on the bridge had suddenly decreased.

Without turning she watched Daugherty study whoever had entered. In the silence some electronic device pipped regularly and the woman—older, her makeup running, the blousy jacket of her stylish, summer suit wilted from ocean spray—sniffled, then uttered a small cry of distress.

"What's she doing here?" Daugherty asked.

Athos's head lolled toward Noreen, his thick eyebrows knitting, "Yes, what *are* you doing here?" He regarded her for a moment. "Ah, now I see—you're enjoying the view." He turned back to Daugherty, "And you should too. Can we get you a chair?" When Daugherty did not reply, he added, "My lady?" and a deck chair was supplied for the woman. She sat.

"What is this?" Daugherty demanded.

Said Athos, "I should tell you this is my boat and I'm captain and I'm just trying to be nice to my guests and you're one. I should tell you I didn't get all this by breaking no big laws of no country, big or small. Bending, maybe, but *breaking?*" He shook his head, then considered his hands. "I had enough of trying to convince people of that, and I don't say nothin' now."

There was a pause before he glanced up at Daugherty. "You got the papers on this Tahgmon or you wasting my time?"

As though confused by the manner in which Athos had broached the subject, Daugherty frowned, then demanded, "My money first."

Athos looked away at the seascape before him. He smiled. "How far you come?" he asked.

Daugherty did not understand.

"Ten miles, twelve. You think you just come twenty miles?" Athos asked.

Daugherty remained impassive, studying the other man.

"You know the Irish limit? Not me. Twenty? Twenty-five miles? You think two hundred? Nah, not two hundred.

"Anyway, far enough you come in that—" Athos leaned forward to look past Daugherty at the speedboat that was dwarfed by the hull of his vessel. "—where you get that thing? What is it?" He paused and eased himself back into the chair, then looked back out at the sea. Finally he added, "You think maybe you're in *my* country now? Here? On this boat?"

When Daugherty still didn't answer, Athos said, "Me neither. And I don't care, except for your navy." He pointed toward the circular screen in front of the helmsman; it was the source of the electronic beeping. "You want that?" He waited, reading Daugherty's expression. "Me neither. Now—you show me what you got."

"I said, the money first."

"For what, your word they're good? The papers. You take my check? Hey—" Athos held out a hand, and the fingers flapped once on the palm.

As Daugherty stared down at it, the wind wailed

through the superstructure. A small muscle flexed on the side of his face. At length, he shook his head once, then dropped his chin onto his chest. Loathedly, it seemed, he unbuttoned the jacket of his tuxedo and pulled out a leather case on which the clover logo of Greenore Eugenics had been embossed. "My mother died for this," he said, handing it to Athos.

"It's not enough," said Athos, quickly zipping the packet open and removing a thick sheaf of paper.

"What d'you mean, not enough? Everything's in those records right from Broadway Moor to"— Daugherty's eyes flickered toward Noreen —"the papers that will get the stallion in your hold into any country in the world."

Without glancing up from the documents, Athos said, "I meant your mother." After studying the first page closely, he then leafed through the rest casually, again perusing the final page before handing it to a man behind him. "Nothing's enough to die for," he observed, as though the thought had meaning in the present context.

Athos then turned his head to the woman. "We never met."

"Machala Walton," she said.

"These your papers?"

She began to nod, but Daugherty said, "They're not hers either."

"More than yours," she shot back.

"Or mine," said Athos, as though musing. He raised an index finger and gestured it at the windscreen. "I wonder —how I know this here horse, these papers, they're right?"

"Because they are!" Daugherty boomed. "That animal with those documents is worth ten million pounds at the inside." Again his eyes moved to Noreen. "And when he was syndicated, that figure was considered a bargain."

"Really?" Athos smiled, as though pleased with himself. He turned to Noreen. "And so cheap. Today I think I have 'a good day,' like they say in America. Nice country, America. Deals there, they're clean. You own, I want. How much? We swap.

"Here?" Athos meant Daugherty. "I don't know *what* he got—ten million pounds of race horse with no name, no papers, breeding horse with no proven foals. Can you believe that? Me?" Athos only looked off at the scene before him, rocking his head slightly, still smiling.

"You ever get in deals like this at your picture gallery?" he asked Noreen, and before she could reply he said, "No —I don't think so.

"Me?" He nodded. "Lots. I get so I like them." He folded his hands in his lap and firmed his shoulders comfortably.

At length Daugherty shifted his feet, his head sweeping the bridge as he turned from Athos and the men beside him to those behind. When he began raising a hand, two stepped forward, one grasping his wrist. The other relieved him of a handgun that was found in a pocket of the tuxedo. They stepped back.

But yet again Athos only waited. After a while, he turned to Machala Walton, "You cold? You want a hot drink? Coffee, tea? Cognac?"

Her eyes searched his face, her own expression suddenly haggard and worn. In the look there was a plea.

"Brandy," said Athos. "Two?" He asked Daugherty, whose chin was again on his chest in a way that both confirmed what Athos had said about his puerility and made Noreen feel for him. He had just admitted to having lost his mother and here too he had lost again.

"You have no intention of paying me?" he asked.

"Paying you for what?"

"For what I own. For what you've taken from me. My horse."

"You? Own? You tell me what you *own?* That horse, which a little bird tells me was stolen? These papers that another little bird tells me are false? Maybe in time they'll turn out to be worth something, but now? They're just a risk and no more—for you, for you.

"I tell you what. Just so you don't starve wherever it is you'll have to go, I'll make you a down payment to show my good faith." Athos raised a hand, and a crewman stepped forward with a folder which he opened. Bound by elasticized clasps were what appeared to be eight bundles of one-hundred-pound sterling banknotes. Athos closed the folder, and reached it toward Daugherty. "If the horse is good, like you say, there'll be more, if you can spend it. That's a promise. Nick Athos is no stiff.

"Now—you got time, hang around. Relax. Maybe you done me a favor. Maybe not." Athos shrugged, "Either way, I don't mind.

"But—" Athos gestured with his chin toward the radar screen. Now two beeps followed by a third were sounding, as the beam swept the horizon. "—maybe you got business." Once more Athos hunched his shoulders, "I can understand why you gotta go.

"George—show Mr. D. to his boat. And give him back that thing he had. Maybe he'll need it to get himself in more trouble."

Flushed, the lips that Noreen had once admired now thin and trembling, Daugherty began to say something but thought better of it when a crewman touched his sleeve. But he paused in front of the woman who did not meet his gaze.

Said Athos, "Maybe it's better you go with him, Miss

Walton. Where I'm headed you'll have trouble without a passport."

"But I don't *want* to leave." Her eyes flashed up to Daugherty. "Not with him."

"Sorry, but you got to."

"What about her?" She meant Noreen.

"This lady's my guest."

Said Daugherty, "C'mon, Machala. We're the only two who know, and we need each other now. There're ways to handle him."

Athos turned to Noreen. "See? What I tell you. He don't have enough trouble. Now he's got to make trouble with me who loves everybody."

Athos stood, as though to accompany Daugherty to the lower deck. A member of his crew had taken a long yellow hose and appeared to be pumping something from the yacht into a tank of the speed boat. "Who will run that farm and your horse business, Miss Walton?"

Said Daugherty without turning to confront Athos, "You're a bastard, know that?"

"A long time. Ten years. Twenty, maybe longer."

"What're they doing to my boat?"

"Fuel. We want you get back, nice and proper. If you're brave you can go the other way." He pointed to the east. "There you can take on the British Navy. They're always ready for a fight."

Daugherty, along with Machala, was escorted to the launch, and for whole minutes—five or ten at least, Noreen guessed—they watched him charge back and forth in the heavy sea, screaming what she assumed were obscenities at the yacht. Machala Walton, hunched down in her seat as though to keep out of the cold, only stared out to sea.

After a while, Athos said to Noreen, "Hey—what I tell you. A boy. You need more proof?"

Perhaps fifteen minutes later, when Daugherty turned and began heading back toward land—slowly now, desultorily, the engine of the launch smoking and hesitating, only to lurch forward for several seconds—Athos explained to Noreen how he planned to return her to land while remaining in what he now staunchly declared were international waters.

13

It was nearly 11:00 when McGarr reached the court house in Wexford. A courier from O'Shaughnessy met him on the stairs with two envelopes. One contained the most recent findings of the enquiries into the two murders. The other, he could see at a glance, was from his wife Noreen.

Ten minutes later he knocked on the door of the chamber of the magistrate, who had just risen from his desk and was accepting his robe from his attendant. "Yes?" he demanded. Then to the attendant, "Who the Christ is he?"

Bald as a post, he was an older man whose skin looked as though it had been scorched in great heat. It was reddened and waxy but as smooth as a baby's. His hazel eyes trained on McGarr for a moment before one splayed radically, canting off toward a corner of the room.

"May I have a word with you?" McGarr asked.

"About what?" the attendant demanded. He was a young man with dark hair, a beetle brow, and a thick line of bushy eyebrows. His face too was red, and McGarr could see that in spite of the heat outside in the sunny square, the room itself was dark and damp. Both men had been sitting near an electric fire.

197

"The Walton matter."

"And you're?"

"Peter McGarr. Gárda Síochána."

Having finally secured the robe on the knobby points of his shoulders, the magistrate pushed the attendant away. "Tea," he said, "and this time hot, damn it."

"But the session? We've a roomful of petitioners. The press."

"And some biscuits. I shan't take tea without biscuits." With a practiced swirl of his shoulders the robe fell to his feet. He batted away the wig. "Now get out," he said to the attendant, who flashed McGarr a bitter, accusatory look as he departed.

The judge then swung his head round, the eyes again training together on McGarr for a moment before the one swung away. "The bloke from the Murder Squad?"

McGarr nodded.

"What can I do for you?"

"A great deal, I hope . . ."

After McGarr explained what he wanted, the official replied, "Apart from clearing off the press, which I'll enjoy, what you ask is in this case not very difficult. You see, there *is* no will. Fionnuala Walton died or, rather, was murdered intestate."

"Which means the next of kin inherits."

"Everything."

When nearly an hour later that news was announced to a courtroom made brilliant by a summer sun that was spangling four arched Georgian windows, silence followed.

McGarr kept his eyes on Siobhan, the elder sister who was sitting in the front row of petitioner seats, directly below the judge's bench. To her left but a significant seat away was her niece, Deirdre, and the intended, Dan Daugherty, whose bluish beard only made the bandage on his cheek seem more obvious.

To Siobhan's right was Mna Daugherty's solicitor, who had earlier explained to the magistrate that in spite of the death of his principal he was representing the interests of her estate. When asked by the court who, specifically, he had replied, "To the best of my knowledge, one Thomas Aloysius Daugherty." None others? "Not to my knowledge." Dan had looked off into the glare, his eyes—it had seemed to McGarr—glassy, his gaze tentative and troubled.

Not so Siobhan's, which remained firmly upon the judge while he searched through a folder of papers. Somehow she had managed to lessen the redness in the injured eye.

"Then from the documents I have before me and by Irish law," he went on, "the elder of the deceased's sisters, Siobhan Emer Burke Walton, is her sole inheritor. Does that satisfy you, Mr. Begley?" he asked the Binn na Rinn Farms solicitor, who had already stood, as if to leave.

McGarr, however, only waited, watching the older woman; he would give her a few moments to enjoy the possibility of her triumph.

Sounds from the crowded hall came to them muffled through a heavy, oak door. Somewhere in Wexford Town a bell was sounding the noon hour. Deirdre had bowed her head, and young Daugherty had remained staring at the windows. The attorney shuffled his feet.

Slowly her eyes moved to the windows and finally fell on McGarr. She blinked.

McGarr boomed to the tall ceiling of the large courtroom which was virtually empty, "She is neither next of kin, nor can a murderess inherit from her victim."

The judge's head snapped up from the papers before him. "I beg your pardon."

McGarr stood, "I said, Siobhan Emer Burke Walton is neither next of kin nor can she inherit from her sister, Fionnuala, whom she murdered."

"Who *is* this man?" the Daugherty solicitor objected.

Producing his Gárda identification, which the court clerk carried to the bench, McGarr did not for a moment take his eyes from the older woman. He was hoping she'd fry in the sear of his gaze.

The judge quickly flipped through McGarr's credentials and motioned the clerk to carry them to the solicitor for his perusal. "You were saying, Chief Superintendent?"

"That the sisters Walton will be busy, your honor. They'll have to answer for a second murder as well. That of Mna Daugherty."

The silence in the courtroom was complete. Even Dan Daugherty had turned his head to McGarr, who now faced Siobhan directly. He spoke out plainly so the court reporter could hear. "The first murder was in a way a crime of passion or, rather, passionate indignation, and it was not without its point. The second murder—in response to what could be viewed as a kind of blackmail—was an attempt to cover up and complete the purpose of the first. But I anticipate myself, wouldn't you say, Siobhan?"

She only closed her eyes and looked away, opening them again when her head had turned to the windows. McGarr paused, gathering his thoughts until the clicking of the stenographer's machine ceased. Behind his back he gently held the injured palm, which felt hot and was throbbing and—he judged—infected.

"You said that on the afternoon just preceding your sister's death, Tom Daugherty remained with you for a while in the kitchen after dinner. Like his younger brother, he sorely desired a chance to press his case with Fionnuala. Not matrimony but rather gain was his object. He wanted to sever the (how shall I call it?) the Taghmon 'breeding program' from any inheritance or settlement or matrimonial gift that she might be thinking of disposing upon the young couple.

"His claim, I suppose, was that he and his father had devoted years of their lives, their sweat and their knowledge of horses to the breeding of this sire line, and that simply turning it over to Deirdre and Dan, who had only just come to work for Greenore Eugenics, was not fair, given all that would be disposed upon them by virtue of whatever Fionnuala was planning to give them for their marriage or the provisions of her estate, as he understood them. Correctly, as it turns out.

"Then, working in consort with his mother and knowing that he and he alone would inherit the lesser but still significant holdings of Binn na Rinn Farms, he had another fiddle to play, though he never got the chance.

"For you, Siobhan, had your own concern about the outcome of the meeting between the two women and— either hearing Mna Daugherty leave or checking to see if she did—you discovered your sister in the attic, poring through her journals and memorabilia. It was then that you confronted her, and you argued. Not long, I'd say, nor —do I think—she knew how vehemently. And you, enraged and morally indignant at having been presented afresh with the embarrassment that had been haunting the Walton family name for forty years and which Fionnuala through Deirdre and Dan was now planning to compound, took her in hand.

"Using your greater size and upper-body strength that your years of manual labor on and about Greenore House had provided, you reached up to the top row of pegs that held Dan, the father's, tools and snatched off the farrier's claw with its sharp head and heavy, forged shaft. You struck her once on the side of the face and again on her left forearm, which she had raised to protect herself.

"And whether those blows drove her from the stairs or, abandoning your weapon, you took her in hand and with one supreme effort cast her from the top, she fell straight to the bottom where she snapped her neck.

"It was then that Tom Daugherty, attracted by the report of her fall or her scream, discovered what had happened, and he paused not. He saw his chance to use the disarray that would inevitably follow Fionnuala's death to make off with the sire upon which she had pinned her hopes for the future of Greenore Eugenics.

"His first mistake, however, was in trying to cover all his bets. In that way he told his mother, whose own 'deal' with the deceased, if she had ever had one, was now over but who perceived yet another opportunity to extract what she wanted—land not horses—from the Walton family.

"Be that as it may, you had left yourself with several problems that, had you acted coolly and without guilt, would most probably have solved themselves.

"First, in the scuffle your eyeglasses had been knocked off and smashed there on the attic floor in front of the trunks. Given the dark day and the poor light from those amber bulbs in the attic, you'd had them on, even though, later, you were to tell me you wore none. Deirdre said you did. As has"— reaching into a pocket of his jacket, McGarr withdrew the several memos that O'Shaughnessy had rushed to him by courier —"Daley, the optician on Wicklow Street. The prescription was written by O'Malley, the ophthalmologist, next door. Three years ago next September." McGarr raised the papers in his hand and shook them.

"It's a slight correction for astigmatism, which allowed you to see well enough without them to clean up most of the pieces but one. Then, you only wore them when reading, and who was to tell? Machala? Not a chance. She had always been envious of Fionnuala for whom she had had to work, and bringing her in on the deed and doubtless the money, for which you yourself with your puritanical, country perspective had little use, would silence her.

"And Deirdre? Well, you went right to work on the plans you had for her, though from little sleep or eye strain or perhaps having been poked by Fionnuala before you dispatched her, only made the redness worse and worse. Early this morning didn't I hear you myself on the telephone. 'That's right, in Wicklow Street,' you were saying to the information operator. Daley, again. Drops he prescribed, to try to clear your guilt.

"But Deirdre was to bear the main burden, wasn't she, since she was so much the cause of what you had done. You decided that right away." McGarr straightened the papers and glanced down at them, though he was merely gathering his thoughts. "And once the decision was made, the details just seemed to tumble right into place, given your knowledge of Greenore House and its contents.

"I'm not certain of the sequence, but handily you'd already sent Deirdre on what she herself described as a 'fool's errand,' for a few supplies in Kilranell. You'd even gone as far as asking Fionnuala to ask her. And having known all along what was afoot—after all, the place is . . . *was* your world entire—you'd made sure she was out of the way when you confronted your sister about what you considered the enormity of her intentions. A quiet woman, for years you had guarded your opinion and sub-

203

mitted to Fionnuala's—shall I call it suzerainty?

"But here you judged her more than simply wrong, as, you believed, she had been often in the past. What she was now planning to aid and abet was morally abhorrent and contravened the basic proscriptions of society, and to it you would not allow her to lend the family name. Then, even if unknowing, wasn't Deirdre a party to the intention? Born in shame, Deirdre was by this planned marriage only compounding what you perceived as the ignominy that Fionnuala had brought upon the family.

"But what to do? Would Fionnuala's fall be considered an accident or would it be investigated for what it was? Accident would have been my guess, but murderers always try too hard, and you were no different. Down to Deirdre's room you went, knowing that the rags she used to weatherize her boots and training tack would be covered with dubbin, which would both clear away the dust and the tracks of your scuffle and leave a film that could be traced to the tin of the stuff that was in her room.

"And once having decided upon that course, the prying up of the rug with the farrier's claw and then the cleaning of the tool and leaving it where Deirdre, who was due soon and because of her affection for the woman she knew as her 'aunt,' would pick it up, followed rather naturally, did it not? You knew that she'd be interested in whatever might have transpired between 'Fi,' as she called her, and Mna Daugherty and then her Dan and Tom—one family with three petitions and each motive enough for murder? Wasn't that enough for you too? Why, then, attempt to throw suspicion upon your niece?

"For you the answer was plain. She was the reason you had murdered, was she not? And you did not have to think. The passion—with which you had killed—was still upon you, and you merely reacted to it.

"The dust behind the door?"

McGarr canted his head and touched a finger of his good hand to an eyebrow. He was sweating now, worrying the details, working for a confession. He would present her with every scrap of evidence he had at the risk of jeopardizing any future case, knowing full well how important any admission here might prove. With a court reporter, a judge, and several experienced observers looking on, the setting could not be more advantageous. He again thought of his wife before he bent his mind back to the task.

"I can't decide if leaving it there, where Deirdre would not look but others would, was an inspired omission or merely luck. It was telling, all right, but perhaps too much so. Would somebody who had taken such pains with the farrier's claw and the dust in the other parts of that attic then 'step' in that wedge? Perhaps, if rushed or understandably harried by her own fears.

"But why, then, would Deirdre—if she had committed the crime—have left three fingerprints on the weapon, which she had already cleaned. And why, if she had grabbed up the claw in the heat of an argument or a tussle to strike her 'aunt,' why had she then been unable to hang it back on its hook correctly. More to this point, by what means had she, who is at most five feet in height, wiped dust from the walls at least a foot above the topmost hooks? And why? Had her hands somehow come in contact with that part of the wall?"

McGarr shook his head. "No. And she, of all of you, would have been least likely to have then rifled through the journals of years up to twenty-plus before she was born to remove a yearbook here and a page there. And then to have cut with scrupulous (shall I say *loving?*) care, the record of marriages, births, and deaths of the last

205

century of this family, as if—to the unobservant—those events had never been recorded. Why? It was less her history than everybody else's, including the Daughertys, who were in every other way but by marriage wedded to Fionnuala Walton and Greenore House.

"And to you, a house-bound crone who had little else but silence and dust, expurgating that history was of such moment that the very words of those journals remained printed upon your memory. Even when explaining Fionnuala to me *of all people,* you couldn't keep from appropriating her language right down to the phrase."

McGarr himself now glanced up at the windows. It was of enough moment to him that he too remembered the words, " '. . . the wailing, the crying from the hedges, the hills, as though from some poor, dying, defenseless thing. . . .' And the phrase, '. . . desperate and pitiable in its sound.' Her words and *your* words and different enough that there can be no doubt where you got them, written as they were forty years ago.

"For it was you"—McGarr lowered his head to her—"who went through those journals and extracted the book for the year 1966. You, who with straightedge and razor blade cut the final page of births, deaths, and marriages from the family Bible. Why?"

McGarr waited until at great length she finally allowed her eyes to move away from the windows and meet his. Whatever she had used to help purge her eye of its redness was wearing off. The corner was now bright pink and looked like the palm of his injured hand felt—hot and throbbing.

"Because your sister Dympna had died in Leeds in 1964, two years before Deirdre's birth. Because you knew Fionnuala had made no will and Deirdre here was really *her* child. The journal of her birth year and the Bible page

206

would have proved that out, wouldn't it, and so that information had to be destroyed no matter how difficult you found the task.

"What?" Deirdre demanded, as though only now comprehending what McGarr had said.

He passed young Daugherty the copy of the information O'Shaughnessy had handed him. Daugherty handed it to the young woman.

"And Mna Daugherty? She was killed simply because she knew. Her having 'forged a deal' with Fionnuala, as she claimed, proved as much, and, after your sister's death, her siccing the local lads on you only pointed up the fact. Whether she paid them in money or drinks or divulged the fact of Fionnuala's death and claimed you two were responsible or, more likely, made up some apocryphal story was not important, since she would never have told anybody your real shame without using it to her own end first.

"Which was? Walton land. What to Fionnuala, with her horses and her breeding program and her mind filled with the forthcoming marriage, was not essential. But for you two aging crones, it was all that had ever given your lives point.

"Didn't I myself hear Mna on the phone with you an hour or two before her death, saying, 'Me? It's just some of the lads poking fun, is all. Sure, I always said, what's good for horses and cattle must have some application to family life. I'm only wanting a bit for me own. Tomorrow will be as good a time as any to patch things up.' Here, she meant. Here in this courtroom or perhaps out in the hall or some alcove, which was more her style. She knew she had you, and she knew too much.

"You *two* old crones?" McGarr repeated, his gaze and Siobhan's still locked. "Certainly—for you in your condition, barely able to climb the stairs, having to pause and use a handrail, could not have stolen down the lane to Binn na Rinn Farms and searched out and slain Mna Daugherty while she dozed in her rocker. That was Machala's contribution, which would bind her to you and *your* money. Machala who likes fancy things—clothes and cars. Machala, who would have needed the struts of the rocker to make up for any strength she lacked. Machala, who would have tied a square knot.

"For you and she were the only two whose presence wasn't accounted for at the time. Deirdre was with me down at the horse barns and Dan, while in transit to his mother's house, was both injured and being harried by the blowers and could not have made it on time. Tom? He was about his bit of 'horse business,' I should imagine, out on Carnsore Point. In any case, he was being watched." McGarr only hoped. He glanced at his hand then looked back up at Siobhan. It was time, he judged, to call for her card.

"Then we have a witness to her presence there," he elaborated. "A man who is as familiar with the farmhouse there as you are with your own, and I use this forum here to charge you with the murder of your sister, Fionnuala, and complicity in the death of your neighbor, Mna Daugherty." Turning to the judge, he added, "I hope the court so notes."

The judge, who seemed to well understand McGarr's ploy, only nodded and turned back to the woman.

And they waited, while the niece kept glancing from one slip of paper to another and then up at McGarr. Pigeons could be heard cooing at the eaves of the building.

Finally Siobhan lowered her eyes to her large, pink hands. In them she held a pair of black gloves. "Why?" she asked in a small voice.

"I beg your pardon?" the magistrate asked. "The court cannot hear you."

"I said why? For this record that he appears to be making here, I want him who knows so much to tell everybody *why* I murdered my own sister."

Said McGarr, "Because of what she told you she would not only make sure would happen but would also sponsor with all of her—and your—resources, in that way making you a party to the . . . is *project* too strong a term?

"Because of what she told you there in the attic, which she had told Mna Daugherty earlier and Mna told me: that in spite of what you and she and Mna knew about Deirdre's birth, Fionnuala was planning to endorse Deirdre and Dan's marriage. That she looked upon the planned alliance as she would upon the mating of two of her animals.

"That far from acknowledging the proscriptions that society has placed upon in-breeding in humans, Fionnuala was elated at the possibility of enshrining Dan's good qualities. Said Mna to me, 'She showed me this chart, just like down at the Eugenics, but instead of having horses on it, it had people. She kept going on about Dan and how prepotent she thought he'd prove. She even began speaking of Dan and Deirdre's get.'

"Mna herself had her own project, which took precedence over all else and allowed her to turn a blind eye. But you? What had you but your name, which by the mating of half brother with half sister would be sullied beyond any mere marriage of your sister to a man who had already gotten another woman with child. It was another but far more detestable shame that would again make your family the object of derision of the county.

"And by whom? Fionnuala once more, who had not merely taken that same, then-married man to her bed but

209

had had the audacity to have his child and bring her back here under the lie that the baby was Dympna's, who was dead. Fionnuala, whom Machala had called a 'domineering bitch who wanted to control everything, even natural processes' and blamed for allowing the Daughertys to assert what she called a 'hegemony' over Walton holdings.

"You could not allow that to happen, and when Fionnuala, ebullient as she had been with Mna Daugherty, spoke glowingly of the prospects of such an alliance, those hands of yours, which had labored for her and Greenore House and the Walton family name for your entire life and are still strong, took over. Either using the farrier's claw or your greater size you pulled her to the brink of the stairs and, like some archangel, cast her down.

"You who characterized yourself to me as having led the good life, 'injuring nobody, incensing none.' You who in raising Deirdre had shown her 'right from wrong.' Could you let what Fionnuala was planning happen to her unknowing? Could you preside over what you viewed as the further destruction of the Walton family name?

"Your words," said McGarr in conclusion. "Your motive."

There was yet another long pause in which a hand moved and gently closed her left eye. The finger remained on the lid for a few moments. Her head then nodded once. "You have it."

McGarr glanced away at Deirdre and Dan, who now possessed so much and so little. Daugherty had held out his palm, in which she had placed her hand. They were staring down at them.

"Excuse me?" the judge said. "I would like that said louder. For the court."

But Siobhan had again raised her eyes to the windows.

14

From the bridge of the cutter *Emer*, Ward possessed an unequaled view of the Irish Sea, yet he still could not see the vessel that he now knew was Nick B. Athos's *Amphitrite* nor either of the two much smaller boats which had left it.

As the captain of the *Emer* had just explained, one of the small boats was either having some sort of engine trouble or was being operated erratically. It was spurting ahead toward Tuskar Rock, only to halt abruptly. A man was at the wheel, and there was a form slumped down in the other cockpit seat that a reconnaisance pilot guessed was a woman.

The second small boat, which had only minutes before departed from the *Amphitrite*, contained a woman. At the tiller she had pulled back the hood of a parka and waved to the plane when it dipped low. Her hair was red, and Ward was relieved.

At this second departure, the *Amphitrite* had wheeled suddenly and was now driving east toward the shipping lanes of the Irish Sea at a speed that would soon put it out of reach of the *Emer*. "I don't know what that vessel has for power," the captain now explained, "but it's significant. What speed is she doing now?"

"Just over forty-five knots, sir," a crewman replied. "Forty-seven. Forty-eight."

"My God," said the captain. "We've not a hope in hell of catching her."

It was then that the burst of light starred the windscreen of the *Emer*'s bridge and, seconds later, a shock wave seemed to stagger the heavy vessel.

"What was *that?*" the captain demanded.

An officer pointed to the radar screen. "It must have been that first boat, the one with the engine trouble." One of the two lights had vanished from the scanner.

In the launch that Athos had given her, saying, "When you get to shore sell it or, better, keep it as a memento," Noreen flinched at the fireball and felt the concussion, like a punch, on her face. A wave of heat followed and then bits of debris, and she looked back, thinking at first that the *Amphitrite* had exploded. But she could hear the vessel, and on the crest of a wave just see it now at the horizon.

She was only a sometime sailor, however, and she bent her attention to the compass and the bearing Athos had advised her to assume. He had also said, "And who knows when your ship might come in? I give you a tip. Two, three years' time, make yourself a promise. Bet on everything by Taghmon or whatever his name will be.

"There'll be the flurry in the papers, the magazines, but only you, me, and the others there on Greenore Point will know for sure. By that time they'll have their own or something close to it, and they won't say nothin'.

"You? *You* write the book. First off, nobody'll believe it —how could somebody import such a horse into any country anywhere? Well, I ain't just somebody, and I began in this boat business smuggling, like my father. Papers? They're easy to come by too.

"And pretty soon? With all the talk, you become the expert. You could retire on that and forget art pictures and"—he had waved a hand and looked toward the west —"crime.

"Hey—I want somebody who can say it to know."

That just before she shoved off.

A week and a day later at Frenche Park Manor in Dunlavin, County Kildare, Noreen again found herself in the company of William Crane and Edward Hopper. Like biddies strolling through a neighborhood or, here, motoring through the horsing country of Ireland, they were making the rounds of those farms and estates at which they knew they would receive a warm welcome. And with the papers still filled with the arraignment and judicial details of what were now being called the "Greenore Point Murders," they could not have kept themselves away.

Hopper was saying, "I knew when I saw you on that blasted Spaniard's boat with that Daugherty fellow the other night you and Peter were up to something."

"It was good of you not to have let on," said Noreen, touching her teacup to her lips.

"Greek," said Crane, who was seated across from her, wearing half-boots, twill trousers, a houndstooth jacket, a beige vest and a regimental tie. In short, The Uniform, she thought, placing the cup in its saucer on the table before her and turning to the fire. It had become glowery again.

"*What?*" demanded Hopper, his eyes bulging as his wire-brush moustache twitched. Dressed like his friend though in slightly different colors, he had adopted a military pose by the mantel, legs spread, one hand behind his back as though at "parade rest." In the fist of the other, which was held at belt level, he grasped bravely the immense whiskey that Noreen's father had poured before shunting them off on her with the excuse that some mare or other needed tending.

"The fellow's Greek," said Crane, raising his glass.

"Daugherty? He is—or, rather, *was*— like hell. They'd been there on Greenore Point since Year One. The Daughertys. Still are, the surviving son, or so said the *Times*, if you can trust it and I don't. Bloody stuffy literati. There was a po-em in there the other day that had no more to do with nothing than anything I've ever read. What this country needs is a little more discipline and less —"

"Not Daugherty, *Athos*," said Crane in a wearily tolerant tone.

Hopper blinked. He glanced down at his whiskey and swirled the tumbler. "Who's he?"

"I thought you said you read the write-up in the *Times*. And here we're after having just spoken of being on his boat. The three of us."

And so it went for what seemed to Noreen like hours, until, their speech began to glide and it was too late not to invite them to stay for the leg of lamb that was appreciable whenever the door to the hallway to the kitchen opened. It was then that Hopper finally broached what they had come about. "You know all that rubbish you asked us aboard the boat about why Fionnuala might ever have chosen to initiate a breeding program with Taghmon as a sire?"

Said Noreen without looking up from the book that she had begun reading, "I seem to remember something of the sort."

214

"Well, it got Teddy and me thinking, you know, why Fionnuala, who in spite of all that science and whatnot had a good eye for horses and ran a respectable operation there at Greenore Point, why she would have splashed out so much money for a nag like that.

"More surprising still was why on earth she would initiate a breeding program centered on such a lackluster performer with an only acceptable pedigree.

"And finally why—and this is by far the most incredible part—she would squander a bloody fortune on superior mares for the beast when nearly any one of her other studs were by any layman's judgment better bets genealogically than this Taghmon that seems to have disappeared.

"And *disappeared?* Who in the name of ruddy hell would want the plug?" Hopper swirled his drink. Some whiskey splashed out and splatted on the floor.

"Blast!" he roared, and as if angry at the glass, glared from it to Noreen, his eyes liquid from the drink. "Until, *until* it dawned on us who, or rather, *what* this Taghmon looked like in size, shape, color, but most especially markings—the black points, the stockings to the cannons, the white blaze on the forehead right down to the nose."

There was a long, dramatic pause in which Noreen turned a page in her book and glanced at her watch to check the nearness of the supper hour.

It rather took the edge off the word that Hopper now said, as though uttering the answer to the riddle of the Sphinx. "Shergar!"

Noreen turned another page. She reached for her teacup, which she touched to her lips and set down. Pretending to have suddenly become conscious of the silence, she looked up from her book and said, "I beg your pardon. You were saying?"

215

"Shergar," Hopper repeated.

"What about him?"

"Was . . . *could* this Taghmon, as he was called, have been Shergar?"

Noreen lowered the book. She allowed her eyes to drift up from the two men to the great oak beams that tied her father's house. "Shergar? Why?"

"Well—Teddy and I put it together. Apart from the size and shape of the blaze on their foreheads, they were dead ringers, you know. I need not mention that Taghmon was a plug. No real speed. None at all over distance." Hopper looked off, and Noreen allowed the silence to carry his question.

"I mean," he went on after an uncomfortable pause, "it would have been the ideal ploy and rather handily accomplished, we concluded. The Ballymany Stud isn't all that far from here." He meant the Aga Khan's breeding farm from which the horse had been stolen. It was about the same distance from Greenore Point as her father's farm —forty or fifty miles.

"Then, one would merely have had to have hired some bully boys—or, better, given the gang of them there at Greenore Eugenics—arranged to have everybody done out in IRA mufti, as it were. You know, some carbines, some automatic weapons. Have somebody give out with some Belfast or Derry gaff and let it slip that they were some of the 'lads,' you see.

"The Paris phone calls?" Hopper meant the series of telephone calls that had been made from Paris to Gárda operatives, who without the knowledge of French authorities had tried to arrange the return of the animal. Nothing had come of them, and when the French police had learned what had transpired, they had been outraged. The Shergar incident remained one of the darker recent moments of the Gárda Síochána.

"They were just an attempt to put people off the idea that the horse had remained all the while right here in Ireland.

"And the other supposition—that somehow somebody had had the . . . unmitigated callousness to say nothing of sublime ignorance to have dispatched such a glorious beast is beyond belief. One look—a *glance*—at that magnificent animal would be enough to melt the heart of any killer, I should imagine."

Noreen sharpened her gaze and took in the figure of the former Justice who was now rocking in place, staring down at the glass in his hand. Color had seeped into his face. "And what a cover," he went on. "Greenore Eugenics and Miss Fionnuala Walton, Pee, Haitch, Dee. One needed only to brown out a bit of the blaze and snuggle the nag into the stud and enough said. Of course Taghmon himself would have had to have been gotten rid of. No wonder she stuck it when that American woman was bidding up the price at the Ballsbridge auction. Everybody thought Fi had gone off her knob, and there all along she was merely purchasing a 'cover,' so to speak.

"Then, that would explain all the buying and breeding with foals from Charlottesville and Sybil's Niece. With Shergar it would have been inbreeding at its very, very best but with Taghmon—a terrible waste of good blood.

"And speaking of blood—it would account for the 'Wexford Murders' as well. I mean, girl, who the devil would kill not once but twice for Taghmon, whereas, Shergar . . . ?" Hopper's voice tailed off. He firmed his drink against his paunch and regarded her. Throughout the entire (was it?) proposition, Crane had not taken his eyes from Noreen's face.

"You know, that very thought occurred to me," she said

in a speculative tone, while easing her feet to the floor and gathering the book, as though to stand. "But, sure—how could one know with Fi and Tommy and poor Machala all gone now. Even this Taghmon can't be found."

"Did you know them *that* well?" Crane asked.

Noreen only canted her head. She smiled. "I think I'll give Peter a shout," she said, rising from the sofa.

"Yes, do. Have you ever spoken to him about it?"

"About what?" She was halfway to the door.

"Why, Shergar, of course," Hopper blurted out. "Those people had him there on Greenore Point all the while, while your husband and his tribe were thrashing all over the Continent like fools. The least you can do is set the record straight."

How, Noreen thought? And at what bother and expense, when Athos would only move the animal or destroy it? Then, the investigation had not—thank God—been the responsibility of the Murder Squad and was, she suspected, a bog best left unplumbed. And finally, Athos had been right. Her knowledge would provide her with at least several opportunities.

As if tired with the talk, she sighed and reached for the handle of the door to the hall.

"Where is Peter, anyway?" Crane asked in a conciliatory tone, checking the level in his glass now that she was on her feet. "Upstairs?"

No, she thought, he had conveniently absented himself from Dunlavin, and the farm. "He's at the Richmond, actually," she replied. "Or at least he should be." It was a noted Dublin hospital. "You know, within striking distance of Hogan's."

It was a noted Dublin pub.